# FLIGHT TO GLORY

By the Same Author . . .

*Doctor to Africa*
*Hidden Valley*
*When the Bamboo Sings*
*Beyond the Tangled Mountain*

# FLIGHT TO GLORY

by Douglas C. Percy

ZONDERVAN PUBLISHING HOUSE
GRAND RAPIDS, MICHIGAN

DEDICATED TO
MERLIN GROVE, B.Th.
martyred in Somalia, July 1960
and
DOROTHY GROVE,
loving wife and brave widow.

"CHRIST SHALL BE MAGNIFIED IN MY BODY,
WHETHER IT BE BY LIFE, OR BY DEATH."

# FLIGHT TO GLORY

## BY WAY OF INTRODUCTION

It was July 16, 1960, when the long distance call reached me. News had been flashed from Somalia, in East Africa, that the Rev. Merlin Grove had been assassinated by a fanatical Muslim, while registering students for a Mission school. His wife Dorothy had been seriously wounded by the assassin, and was in a hospital, dangerously ill.

Merlin was one of my students at the Toronto Bible College, and we had often counseled and prayed together regarding his life work. Being an older student, he was a close friend and a brother beloved in the Lord.

With his wife Dorothy, he had been sent to Somalia by the Mennonite Board, and for two years had labored long and well. Fruit was beginning to show. Now he was dead.

Shocked, I made my way to his home to bring my personal condolences and sympathy to his parents. Mrs. Grove, Sr. saw me coming and walked towards me. She stood silent for a moment with tears filling her eyes, then she reached up and took the lapels of my coat in her hand. Looking into my eyes she said simply: "We weep, Mr. Percy, we weep in our hearts, but we have no regrets. We would rather have Merlin lying in a grave in Africa in the will of God than be strong and hearty at home, disobeying Him."

I had little to say in the face of such faith and courage. "God doesn't make any mistakes," I said. "I don't know why Merlin had to die, but God does. One day we will know why."

Some months later, I paid a visit to the hospital where Dorothy had undergone a spinal fusion, the result of the attack. I walked into the room bracing myself to face the widow with her loss and to console her as a brother in Christ.

As I walked in, I noticed that she was lying face down on a stryker frame. On hearing me approach, she turned a radiant, smiling face towards me. Her greeting was warm, her joy evident and her courage high. I found myself with tears coursing down my cheeks as she told of the death of her husband. "I don't know why God has honored us in this way," she went on. "I feel so unworthy. But I know that Merlin has not died in vain. Nothing we give to Jesus Christ is too great, nor is it a sacrifice. We both loved Him," and again her radiant smile.

Since that time I have often seen the parents and the widow and they are always the same: radiant, courageous, and trusting God. I have not been able to get away from their witness and steadfastness, and when writing this story, felt that it should center around this event that must redound to the glory of God. For that reason, it is woven in with a story that we trust will challenge and inspire the Christian youth of today to a high and holy calling in Christ Jesus our Lord.

Douglas C. Percy

*Toronto Bible College,*
*Toronto, Canada.*

# I

The little Piper Pacer slipped sideways in the uprush of warm air. Looking like a giant yellow moth, the plane stood out in bold contrast to the steel blue of the sky above, and the dense green mist of the African jungle below.

At the controls, a heavy set man slumped in familiar ease in the tiny cockpit that he seemed to fill. A baseball cap was pulled low over eyes that swept restlessly over the terrain beneath, then switched to the instrument panel in front of him. Almost by instinct rather than actually reading the dials, he noted his air speed, altitude, oil pressure and gas gauge. His cockpit ease belied the alertness of the man who knows that he is living in a foreign environment, and an unguarded or careless moment might bring irretrievable disaster.

The features of the man were not unusual. They were neither handsome nor plain. The forehead was wide and smooth. A generous nose gave a slightly hawklike appearance to the deeply tanned face. He was no grim-faced man. The mouth, with lower lip jutting slightly beyond the upper, showed many wrinkles at the corners, hinting at a ready smile that often creased his face. It was the mouth of the man in love with life to whom laughter came as easily as breathing. It was the look of the man who saw humor in everything, or who manufactured it when it was absent.

This was no mere comedian, however. The over-all appearance was of a man, strong, confident, perhaps arrogant, as characterizes a man who has *slipped the surly bonds of earth, and danced the skies on laughter silvered wings.*

One tanned hand grasped the control stick, the other moved automatically to the instrument panel in front of him. His feet rested lightly on the rudder bar, moving ever so slightly as his body, one with the machine, sensed the drift and pressure of the plane.

His eyes continued to dart to and fro as though seeking to pierce the green mass of jungle below.

Suddenly something caught his eye, and he shifted the rudder bar a trifle, while his plane, like a well trained horse responding to the light pressure of bit and bridle, banked slightly to the left.

What had caught his eye as a faint glimmer now became increasingly clear. The plane slowly descending in its wide arc, broke away from the mass of jungle to show a clearing off to the east.

Soon the clearing was directly below him and he saw the milling of the small group of people almost directly below his plane, while the pattern of the compound stood out in bold relief against the jungle that surrounded it.

The metal roof of a large, square building reflected the sun as he skimmed over it, then it slipped past, and he was over another building from whose door he saw two figures emerge, and with hands shading their eyes, squint skyward.

With a grunt of satisfaction the pilot noticed the white man and woman as they waved in that inane fashion of people to whom the sight of a plane is strange, and who wave as though expecting to see a hand wave back.

As he put his plane into a tight spin to circle the compound once more, the pilot opened the small window near his left shoulder and with admirable negligence waved back to the people on the ground, chuckling as he did so.

With the plane in its circle, he switched on the automatic pilot. Then from his breast pocket, took pad and pen, and swiftly wrote a note.

He took a small plastic bag and slipped the note and several small lead weights into it. Reaching down to the floor of the cockpit he picked up a plastic bucket with a long rope attached to the handle.

He placed the note in the bucket, then slipped the bucket out the window, saw it caught in the slipstream, and held it there. Once more he took over the control, and this time put the plane into a steeper bank still until one wing was pointing almost at right angles to the ground. As the plane banked the bucket dropped down alongside the door, and with his one free hand the pilot began to play out the rope, his eyes noting that the knot of people below were the exact center of his circle.

Swinging only slightly like a giant pendulum, the bucket dropped lower and lower, as with consummate skill the pilot kept his plane in its perfect circle. *It's like dropping a bucket into a well*, he thought with satisfaction. The rope was attached to the handhold on the far side of the cockpit, and the pilot saw that the rope was nearly played out. On his next circle he dropped the plane down another hundred feet, still with his eyes on the bucket and on the trees that were closing in on him. He saw the hands of the man below reach up for the bucket, miss it as it gyrated slowly out of his grasp, then plop on the ground almost at his feet, and keel over on its side.

"Bull's eye," whispered the pilot to himself with a grin of self satisfaction, then turned his attention to his plane, keeping it rotating on the end of the long rope, scarcely moving the bucket as he did so.

With a sigh of relief, the man in the plane saw the hand signal and the immediate action on the ground. Still circling the plane, he slowly drew up the bucket and pulled it in through the window. Straightening the plane out, he pulled back on his control, watched as the plane nosed above the trees, gave it full power, and felt the sudden pull as the propeller gripped the fast rushing air. Soon he was above the trees, the people below had shrunk to pygmy size, then the edge of the jungle blotted them from sight.

Swinging around he picked out the serpentine road, then followed it for the ten miles or so that he had checked on before. He picked out the landmarks that he had impressed on his memory, saw his straight clear stretch, and with infinite skill he sifted down the narrow valley that the road made in the jungle, gauged the distance perfectly and gently set the wheels down on the uneven surface. A series of short hops, a bump, and the plane moving smoothly along was gradually slowed by the brakes, then rolled to a stop. The door swung open, the legs of the pilot appeared, one foot waved about feeling for the L shaped step, then the rest of the body followed and the man dropped to the ground. Tilting his cap to the back of his head the pilot looked around with the curious gaze of a man interested in anything he saw, checked the area for takeoff, then leaned with his back to the fuselage to wait.

*So this is the Africa of Peter Dunning,* he thought to himself. *I wonder if it is all he says it is. Guess I'll soon find out,* and folding his arms he focused his eyes on the road and waited.

# II

Bill McAdams looked at his wife across the remains of their breakfast, and laughed. "You and your dreams," he chided, "you should know that there is no relation between what crosses your mind at night while you sleep and what crossed your path in the morning when you are awake."

"I don't care," she said, "it was so real that I just *know* something is going to happen today. Didn't God speak to men in the Old Testament through dreams?" she threw at him suddenly. Then without waiting for a reply, she went on, "You watch, something. . . . . . ." her voice trailed off, her eyes grew wide, as through the screen door there came a faint hum that had no relation to any other noise that should be heard on that hot morning in Africa. The clamor of voices outside did not drown out the humming sound that seemed to grow louder and louder.

"It's a plane," she shouted, and like a girl, and without waiting for a reply from her husband she flung herself away from the table and out the door.

Her husband was right behind her and they burst through the door as a little yellow plane broke out of the early morning haze, and began to circle the compound, dropping lower and lower as it did so.

Almost by reflex action the two on the ground raised their hands in a waving salute, their eyes fixed on the plane that seemed so small against the great expanse of sky above.

They watched the pilot bank into a tight turn, saw a small window slide back and a bucket appear at the end of a rope.

Then as the plane seemed to fix its circle immediately around them, they saw the bucket slowly lower, dropping foot by foot with only a slight pendulum motion until it touched the ground immediately in front of them with a thump, then spilled over on to its side.

"Now will you believe in my dreams?" she couldn't help asking, as they ran to the spot where the bucket was lying. She felt somewhat sheepish at her insistence that dreams were omens and signs. She knew better than that. It was just that the dream had been so vivid.

Dr. Bill McAdams had moved quickly to the bucket, and holding it with one hand as though fearful of losing it, he dipped into it with the other, pulling out the weighted, plastic packet.

"What is it, Bill?" the woman at his side asked impatiently, looking first at the packet and then at the plane, whose pilot could be seen through the open window, gesturing to them. "Hurry up, he wants you to open it."

The doctor quickly opened the packet and pulled out the note. With his wife looking over his shoulder, he read:

"Dear Dr. McAdams: Pardon me for coming in for breakfast unannounced, but I am most anxious to meet you and Mrs. Mc-Adams. Unfortunately, this is no whirly bird, and you have no runway. I can land on your so-called road about ten miles west of here. If you could meet me there with a conveyance of some sort (with my sort of luck it will be a horse! But then I hate walking too!), I will be glad to accept your breakfast invitation (you gave me one, didn't you?) and come back with you. Perhaps you could bring someone along to guard the plane for me. Anyway, I have to see you since I have a message from Peter Dunning, and he told me (a) I had to deliver it personally, and (b) that I had to do it as quickly as possible. This is it, and here I am. Wave your hand if it is o.k. Over and out.

Alan Volkes."

The man on the ground looked up at the circling plane, **waved** one arm, and with training born of emergencies he spoke quickly to his wife, barked an order for his horse to one of the African men standing by, then ran back to the house to get into his riding gear.

"A message from Peter," he said to his wife as she hurried to keep up with him. "That fellow is full of surprises," he added with enthusiasm. "Wonder if it's about the possibility of him getting back here?" and he asked the question somewhat wistfully.

It did not take him long to change, then with a wave of his hand to his wife, he headed for the back end of the compound where he saw two horses restless and rearing being held by his friend Baru and one of his sons.

It took him only a moment to get into the saddle. The horse was still restless from the unusual noise from the sky and it took him sometime to quieten him down. Then he looked down at his wife.

"I'll leave Baru to watch the plane and bring this fellow Volkes back with me on Baru's horse," he grinned down at her. "Guess I'll have to do more dreaming," his eyes were mischievous as he looked at this lovely little woman who shared his missionary life with such courage. Suddenly he was grabbing for the pommel of the saddle, as she gave the horse a great smack with the flat of her hand, that nearly caused her husband to unseat.

With the wind whistling in his ears, and his short cropped, dark hair lifting slightly in the breeze that the gallop created, McAdams settled himself in the saddle with the ease of long experience and gave himself up to the joy of speed, the delight of racing through the towering jungle that was thoroughly wakened by the noise of the plane, and now the additional noise of the rapid pad of the horse's unshod hooves echoing among the trees.

Lazy lizards, heads momentarily cocked at this new sound, suddenly scurried off to the safety of the tall grass. Twice, chattering monkeys fled from a silent contemplation of their furred bellies, and swung to the safety of the trees.

The ease of saddle slump made horse and rider one, and knowing that Baru was riding almost as quickly behind him, he gave himself up to pondering the new twists in the life he had chosen as a medical missionary in Africa. The news that filtered down from the north was almost frightening, and an air of revolution was in the land.

Isolated in his own area he seemed shut off from the rest of Africa and the rest of the world. But Baru had been telling him of the restlessness that must soon penetrate even this remote area.

*Oh well, we are bound to see changes these days,* he thought. *The winds of change have surely been blowing strongly in this beautiful but uncertain country as in other parts of the world.*

Mentally he ticked off the changes that he had seen. Independence and all the frustrations of unfamiliar government and power had made the air tense. The rise of some politicians of ability and depth, and the power hungry reach of others who saw only their own advantage and profit, had pulled the country apart and divided its people. He had heard about the reawakened tribal jealousies, the increased antagonism of the Muslim community, and all the attendant restlessness of an emerging people.

And down at the grassroots, he had seen the bewilderment of the people, slowly awakening to a twentieth century with which they were unprepared to cope, who were becoming the pawns of some, the burden of others.

Interwoven with it all, he had heard of the tribal jealousies, the ferocious religious antagonisms, much of it slanted at the Christian church and many of its missionaries, whose greatest fault was that they came from the unknown but maligned western world, and whose acts of love and mercy were being constantly misconstrued, to become the springboard for power hungry ambitions.

McAdams wondered where it would all end. "In the meantime," he soliloquized, "I've got a job to do and I'll do it as long as I can." It was just that sometimes it seemed such a thankless job. Bill pounded the saddle horn in frustration, and suddenly found himself clutching that same horn in an almost amateurish attempt to keep himself from going up the horse's neck and over its head.

With its fore hooves digging into the hard packed soil, the horse shied off to the right, with the rider's head snapping in a violent whip lash that had come so unexpectedly mid stride of the flowing motion of the horse's pace. The rider fought for control.

All the time, while it backed and reared, the horse would cast a frenzied eye at something it had seen on the road ahead. As he fought for control and the animal gradually stopped its frenzied threshing, Bill saw what had caused it all. The tail assembly of the little plane was poking out from a bend just ahead, and leaning against it, with a grin on his face, baseball cap pushed back on his head, was the pilot.

Bill suddenly remembered Baru who would be pounding along behind him and might at any moment come upon this scene. With a loud "Halloooooo. . . . *hunkali dai*. . . ." "Helloooooo . . . .take it easy" he made his side-stepping, nervous horse face the direction from which his companion would come.

His warning came a fraction too late. Baru's horse came careening around the bend, its rider frantically sawing at the bit to slow down its headlong rush. Baru saw that he would not be able to stop, took one wild look around, then with the dexterity and skill that was always an amazement to McAdams, he flung himself sideways off the horse, his flailing arms reaching for some of the jungled vines that pushed to the edge of the road. He grabbed one as thick as his wrist, swung off and stood, and was safely on the road while his horse continued its wild, scramble-legged gallop. Too late it saw the tail of the plane, tried to stop and spin away from the terror, couldn't, turned into the bush at the side of the road, and with its momentum unchecked by rein or bit, was hurled into the jungle that engulfed its head, withers and half of its heaving belly before it was stopped.

The rump and rear legs continued to do a series of bucks that sent the doctor and pilot into fits of uncontrollable laughter. With the dark jungle ahead of it, and the monster on the road hidden from its gaze, the animal just stood, as though held in a vise.

"That'll hold her for a while," Bill finally said to Baru, who had joined in on the laughter. He handed his reins to the African, his horse still trying to back away from the plane.

McAdams then walked over to the pilot, who had also recovered himself, and who approached the other with a peculiar loose kneed shuffle. In silence their hands went out in a grip only known to those who meet in the jungle.

It was the same kind of greeting that must have taken place between the aged Livingstone, lost for years to civilization, and the journalist Stanley, who had been sent out by his paper to find the missionary-explorer. History records the latter's "Dr. Livingstone I presume." But no one could record the handclasp of the one who for so long had not seen a whiteman nor heard their common language.

The bony fleshless hand of the missionary would have reached out to be clasped by the strong hand of the man who was to become known as Africa's greatest explorer. For a long moment they would stand thus, while through the fingers and palms would spread the message that the mouth could never form. It would be the touch of friendship and the pushing back of the barriers of loneliness. It would be the touch of strength that only those long denied the touch of a fellow's hand can know and appreciate. And above all it would be the touch of Christian fellowship that needs neither color nor place, words nor sounds, to make itself known. It is a handclasp.

So these two men shook hands in the heart of the African jungle, the doctor and the pilot. Their clasp and the single look that took each other's measure was enough, and they were satisfied.

"I'm Alan Volkes," he said, still gripping the hand of the man whom he had summoned with his bucket message. "And I know that you're Dr. McAdams.

". . . . .Bill," broke in the other.

"Bill McAdams then. I've heard a lot about you, particularly from your friend Peter Dunning, and some others that I have been meeting around the country here. But since this is the first chance I have had to fly over this way, I haven't had the opportunity to meet you or your wife. Jane, isn't it?" he asked.

"Jane," repeated the other.

"And I hear that she is quite an amazing woman," he went on.

"It's true about my wife," he said. "But you will meet her soon. What's the message from Peter?" he went on eagerly. "It's a long time since we have heard from him. Is he coming out soon?" and the question tumbled out in his eagerness to hear.

The other shook his head. "He has been ordered to stay home indefinitely," he said with a tiny shrug, "and if there is a fellow who is restless to get back here again, it's Dunning. But the rest of the news should wait until we get back to your house. Then I can tell you both at once."

# III

The figure lay still in the Canadian hospital bed, held rigid and immobile by the great cast that almost enveloped his body. Even the head, held stiff and straight made no movement.

Eyelids blinked quickly and constantly, seeking in panic to wipe away the fog that had come down so suddenly. He was blind!

The man was Alan Volkes, pilot, scuba diver, spelunker. Name it and he had done it. Anything but stay on the ground, where as he claimed, the chances of getting killed were infinitely better than in the sky, under the sea, or in the bowels of the earth.

"I play it safe," he used to say to his friends who remonstrated with him about flirting with danger and death. "When the odds against my coming out of a plane crash equal the odds of my staying alive in a car accident, I'll fold my wings. But not until," and the jaw that protruded slightly, thrusting his lower lip out would close, and the conversation stop. Then out of his fund of stories and jokes he would twist the moment to a laughing advantage, and his friends would forget that this was the man to whom risk and danger were as his breath.

Now he was immobilized by one of those freak accidents that constantly dog the flight of the pilot of the small plane. A down draft air current, a wildly screaming plane, the sickening crunch of buckling wings, the somersault of the fuselage, and just a whisper between the flyer and death.

"Flying is glorious," he had once said, as he held a group of friends spellbound recounting some of his adventures, larding

22

them with the jokes and quips that were as natural to him as breathing. "Only the last flight is the flight to glory," and he kissed his fingers and flicked them into the air.

Alan Volkes as a boy had been a tinkerer with machinery. The fine, balanced movement of the clock, or the mystery of the internal combustion engine, and all the mechanical things between challenged his precision fingers and the automatic reflexes of the true mechanic's mind. Above all he dreamed of flying.

It was a wonderful age to grow up in. It was a day for planes and cars, rocket propelled jets, and souped-up jalopies. Alan was in his element.

He was not, as he once said himself, "built for speed." His frame was stocky, with a heaviness around the hips that demanded rigid diet control and unending exercise. His youth had been harried by the taunts of others who revelled in slim, youthful figures. He had fought his way through the childhood jungle of thoughtless youth, and had tamed many a youthful namecaller. His independence and self sufficiency had developed the hard way leaving their mark upon the boy and upon the man.

Despite his physique he seemed like one of the planes he was later to handle so ably. He seemed to have the rigidity of framework and strut that would not give way under pressure, yet he was not so rigid that he would snap. There was an easy going calm about him that seemed to ease him through life.

Alan's generation was born for war, and the hopeful pilot early joined his fellow countrymen in the defense of freedom. Turned down as a pilot, he volunteered to service planes, and his skilled hands soon became trained and able to make them safe for others to fly. It was good training, and he was later to be thankful for the providence that forced him to be a mechanic.

After the war he had accepted a friend's offer and entered a broker's office, largely because he could use his time as he would. Wings are restless in folded stillness, and his were widespread for eager flight. He purchased his own plane, then a glider, and lived in the skies, sometimes to the drone of his small Piper Cub, sometimes in the awful silence of the glider that swooped and swung as he followed the air currents along.

Now he was lying immobile and blind with only his inner vision of the places he had once known to save him from despair. The days became weeks.

He would never forget the day, when, after weeks of immobility and blindness he awakened out of a fitful sleep. Faint light made him blink tremulously. Then as though through a fog he saw the faint shape of the window across from his hospital bed and behind it the glow of a new day. Frantically he dug into his pillow and pulled the buzzer that was pinned there. He pushed the knob and held it, somehow feeling that his insistent call must be felt down that hall where the nurses' station was still shrouded in the dim light of the early morning.

A shadow fell across his face. "You want something, Mr. Volkes?" It was the voice of the night nurse.

"Don't look now," replied the irrepressible humorist, "but I can see . . ." his voice broke and he almost shouted, "I can see, I can see!"

The nurse took one look at his face, then turned and raced for the nursing station. "Get a call through to the Doctor, quick," she almost shouted the words as she spun on her heel to go back to the room again. "Number 17 is either delirious or he has had something happen to his eyes." And she pushed back into the room where Volkes was still shouting, "I can see, I can see!"

He could indeed, and day by day his sight improved, as the man began to live again. Soon he was up, uncomfortable and hot in his walking cast, and knowing he looked queer with his rolling gait and stiff torso.

The man who left the hospital was a different man to the one who had gone in. His humor was still irrepressible, and as soon as he could he was flying again, knowing that he had to get back up in the air if he wanted to face life without the heart clutching fear he had known.

But the usual round of work and play now seemed as ashes in his mouth. He often appeared distracted and a far away gleam would come into his eyes. Death had brushed him lightly but it had left its mark.

It was during one of the spells that kept him doodling at his desk, when his friend and business partner, Harry Fromley, came in.

"Alan," he said abruptly, "there's a friend of mine speaking at our Christian Business Men's banquet tomorrow night. Like to go along with me?"

"Sure thing, Harry," the eyes of the man at the desk lost their faraway look. "Be glad to go along. It's a long time since I attended," and he looked apologetic.

"Fine. We can leave from here . . . if you're coming in tomorrow that is," and he grinned at his friend.

"I'll be here," replied Alan with an answering grin.

# IV

The noise that always accompanies a banquet had made Alan's head spin, and his eyes, still sensitive, were beginning to ache. Banquets are all the same. Good food, lots of yattering, special music, a speaker—a deadly sameness. *He was almost sorry that he had come,* he thought. *If it wasn't for good old Harry . . .* he was interrupted by a rapping on a glass.

"Gentlemen. . . . ." the voice of the chairman paused, waiting for the hubbub to die down. "Gentlemen, we're glad to have Mr. Peter Dunning as our speaker tonight. He may not need an introduction to some of you, but let me tell you something about the man who is sitting here on my left."

Alan peered over the heads of the men at his table and saw a tall, fair, almost handsome man sitting at the head table. In contrast to his fair hair, his eyebrows were dark and tended to be bushy. On his face was a slight smile . . . the pleasant look of a man who delighted in this male companionship. Alan liked what he saw and listened for the introduction.

"Mr. Dunning has been a missionary in Africa for a good many years, and at present is at home teaching, helping to train missionaries. Due to some tropical disease he is forbidden to return to his work at present. He has a message that I am sure will touch our hearts tonight. Mr. Dunning."

Alan saw the man rise slowly to his feet until he stood, showing a tall, large frame that seemed to belie any sickness within.

He stood for a moment toying with his water glass and letting his glance sweep around the room with its two hundred men.

"Looks like he's taking stock," muttered Alan to himself, then was somewhat abashed, as the eyes focused on him for a moment and passed on to the rest of his table.

"Gentlemen," the voice rolled out easily, clearly, perhaps slightly too loud as he sought to reach the men at the far end of the room. "I am grateful for the opportunity of speaking to you, man to man.

"When I look at you sitting here after a delicious banquet and in these delightful surroundings," and his hand waved around the room with its quiet but excellent appointments, "I can only think of one thing: there is a potential here, which if linked with the power of God could mean much in this world in which we live."

He paused, and in the slight break, Alan found himself sitting forward on his chair. "Might be what I'm looking for," he said to himself.

"I often wonder if we who profess to be Christians are not satisfied too easily, willing to accept all that God has to offer us by way of salvation, stability, security and peace, but are not ready or willing to enter into all that God has for us.

"Sometime ago we had a speaker at the Bible College who used a phrase that I have not been able to forget. Whatever else he said has gone from my memory, but this I cannot get away from. He said: 'All that God is, is available to the man who is available to all that God is.' Now you can't just hear that phrase and let it go as we do with so many things we hear. I'll repeat it slowly, and as I do, think of what it says." He paused for effect, then repeated it. Alan felt his lips moving in unison as he tried to get the words out with the speaker.

"*All that God is, is available to the man who is available to all that God is.*

"This is what I would like to speak to you about tonight.

"There is an experience for us," he went on, "that is not unlike that of the young wartime aviator John Gillespie Magee when he wrote:

"Oh I've slipped the surly bonds of earth,
And danced the skies on laughter silvered wings,
Sunward I've climbed, and joined the tumbling mirth
Of sun split clouds, and done a hundred things,
You have not dreamed of. Wheeled and soared and swung,
High in the sunlit silence. And hovering there
I've chased the shouting wind aloft, and flung
My eager craft through footless halls of air.
Up, up, the long delirious burning blue,
I've topped the windswept heights with easy grace
Where never lark nor even eagle flew—
And, while with silent lifting mind I've trod
The high untrespassed sanctity of space,
Put out my hand and touched the face of God."

He paused, and Alan's mouth dropped perceptibly open. "That's not poetry, that's experience," he said to himself. "I've felt just like that a hundred times. . . . *'put out my hand and touched the face of God.'* "

Dunning didn't know that he had touched at least one man, and he went on:

"There is an experience with God that is as different to ordinary, subnormal Christian living, as walking in an African jungle is to soaring above it in a jet plane. It is an experience available to all, but it is not known by all. There may be some here tonight who really want to know God in His fullness and availability. If so, it is only on the basis of being available to Him. Perhaps tonight, someone will put out his hand and touch the face of God.

"There is an experience recorded for us, in the life of one of the men of the Bible who really found that all that God is, is available to the man who is available to all that God is. His name is Moses.

"If ever a man experienced and knew the power of God, it was this man. 'What is that in thine hand?' the Lord had asked him on one occasion. It was just a walking stick, a piece of dry and lifeless wood. But touched by God and used by Moses it became a mighty instrument. In many ways the truth of our quotation was proved to Moses and by Moses.

"There is one special time, however, when we see the source and the result of such experience. Moses, like most of us, had just about come to the end of himself. Perhaps that is why you are here tonight. He felt empty, powerless, useless. And in that moment he went up to meet God.

"The Bible tells us that the Lord called him up to the top of the mount. It does not say what happened there, it was a trysting place, a meeting of a man with his God. It does say that something happened to Moses. His face shone with the glory of the experience. But more than that his life became available to the God whom he touched.

"Moses went up the mount alone. He met God alone. He was completely isolated from the stream of humanity, its problems and its needs. He left behind all that he knew and loved and climbed the mountain alone, to meet God.

"The poet said he *slipped the surly bonds of earth*. It is something like that when a man really wants to meet and know God, to find a reason and purpose for his life, and then to fulfill that purpose in the strength that God gives.

"But it is interesting to note this: as soon as Moses had gone up to meet God, the very next verse says: 'Away, get thee down.' Couldn't Moses stay up there and enjoy all that God is? Couldn't he live out his days in that mountain top experience? No, he couldn't. God is not to be selfishly enslaved in the life of one man. He must be shared with others, and there was a whole world of men, women and children waiting for a man such as Moses.

"'Come up and see me,' said God. 'Go down and serve me,' He commanded.

"And with scarcely a sigh, the man of God turned and went down the hill, there to meet again his problems and his people . . . but to meet them with the God he had met, the glory that he had seen, and the new power he had received."

The speaker paused for a moment, then he went on, his voice rich and full, reaching every man who sat in the room.

"And every event in Scripture that records a man being used

of God follows the same pattern. 'Come up and see me, go down and serve me.'

"And I suggest to you men tonight, that what God did for Moses He will do for you and for me.

"He appears to us the God of heaven, the Saviour of the world, our Lord and Master. We see Him dying for us on Calvary, now living for us, and His glory floods our hearts and lives.

"Why? To make us feel good? To prepare us for heaven? Yes, but not only these things but also that His purpose might be worked out through us, and His work done in this world into which He would send us."

The voice of the speaker had been growing stronger and stronger. The sheer weight of words that had come out with trip hammer force and rapidity seemed to fall on Alan. Now the voice dropped down a decibel or two as he continued.

"If you want to know what it means to have all that God is available for you, to fill your life, to give it meaning, purpose and fullness, then you must be available for what He is and what He does.

"I served in Africa. It is one little part of a great world of nearly four billion men, women and children. The world population is exploding so rapidly that scientists wonder if there will be enough food produced for them all by the year 2000 A.D. This is the world for which Christ died. These are the men and women whom He would save. He came into the world and did His part. Now He says, 'as the Father hath sent me, so send I you.' Much of the world still waits for a 'sent one', a missionary.

"The world waits for men and women who have climbed the mountain in a lonely, personal experience, and have touched the face of God in Jesus Christ, only to go out and touch His world for His sake.

"Then come the usual arguments: I'm no preacher, I've had no training, I have other responsibilities. But God only asks two things: 'What is that in thine hand? and, Will you make it available to Me?'

"The first question you can answer easily. The second one is your act of commitment and surrender to Jesus Christ.

"What about you? Ordinary Christian living or extraordinary, rich, full, purposeful living? This is available from God if you are available for God."

The voice stopped. The speaker sat down, and the chairman asked them to bow their heads in silent prayer.

Alan needed that moment.

# V

Alan waited while the men milled around, greeting one another and getting ready to leave the banquet room. At the far end he saw the tall Dunning speaking to some of the men who had pressed forward. He knew that he could never leave the place until he had spoken to him too, but he wanted to do it in comparative privacy.

"Good speaker, isn't he?" Alan looked around to see that Harry was talking to him across the table. "Want a lift home?"

"Thanks, Harry," his voice was somewhat short, "but I wanted to talk to Dunning for a few minutes."

"Oh," his friend noted the solemn look on Alan's face. "That's easily arranged. Come on up and I'll introduce you."

With a slight shrug, Alan followed. This wasn't what he wanted exactly, but he couldn't offend his friend and partner, so he followed him slowly through the crush.

It took them sometime before they were on the fringes of the group that surrounded the speaker.

Peter half turned around at the movement of bodies, and caught sight of Harry Fromley. Excusing himself from the men in front of him, he turned to meet the two. "Harry, it's good to see you," exclaimed Dunning.

"By the way, Peter," said Harry, laying his hand on Alan's arm to pull him into full view, "here's a friend of mine that wants to meet you. Alan Volkes, Peter Dunning.

The two strangers put out tentative hands, and Alan felt his taken in a warm, firm shake, which he returned. "Good to meet you, Alan," said Peter.

Alan hesitated, then despite the men still standing there, he said: "I was interested in what you were saying tonight." He hesitated. "I've done some flying, and I guess you knew how to get the attention of someone who likes to *slip the surly bonds of earth*," and he grinned at being able to remember the two lines.

Peter smiled too.

Alan went on: "I wondered if we could have a talk sometime?"

"Glad to," said Dunning briskly. "Here's my card. Give me a call whenever you're free and I'll be glad to talk to you," then he was claimed by some of the other men.

Harry and Alan turned to leave, the latter wondering what he would talk about if he did follow through his hasty request. He shrugged slightly, and followed his friend out to the car. Perhaps he wouldn't bother. It was just a spur of the moment thing.

The two men drove in silence, the one suspecting that there was something weighing heavily on the mind of the other, and wisely was not intruding.

Alan's mind was back those five years, reliving the most fearful time of his life, and he drew further within himself at the memory of the crash that had brought near death and temporary blindness. A man who brushes death so closely that he can feel it does not quickly forget. And Alan, who had lived so close to the extremes of nature was perhaps more cognizant of God than he had cared to admit. Now he felt afresh the need for an inner satisfaction that so far had eluded him. His mind was in a turmoil.

*He would have to talk to Dunning.*

It was some weeks later that Peter Dunning looked at the man sitting across from him, while the silence grew longer and longer. Alan Volkes was sitting with his chin in his hands, despair written in his whole attitude.

"Ever been on a merry-go-round?" he asked at last, looking up, an air of discontent on his face, his question breaking the silence that had become almost electric.

"Well, that's the way I feel these days. On a merry-go-round, and round and round we go. Not getting anywhere. I just want to get off, to feel I'm getting somewhere and doing something." He looked at the other with a crooked grin. "Whatever it means, I know I want to do something worthwhile," and he slumped back again, the picture of dejection.

Dunning looked at him for a long minute. He had grown to know and love this chubby man, who, despite what he had just said, seemed to have done about everything worth doing. He recalled their earlier conversations after Alan had come to him at the meeting at which he had spoken.

Peter had taken to him almost immediately. Behind the half humorous twist of the mouth he had seen something poignant, an unspoken plea, and subsequently he had put himself out to get near the man.

Peter was thinking of the night when he had asked Alan directly: "Are you a Christian?"

The man had blinked, then smiled. "Harry Fromley led me to Christ about a year ago. If that is being a Christian, I am one. But if there is more to it, then I'm not," he answered with candor.

"It's a good starting point," said Peter. "But it is not the end. The Christian life is a *progressive* thing. Such things as the development of your inner life by prayer and Bible study, the obedience and service you give to God are also a big part in developing into a useful Christian. What most people lack is motivation and availability. They are willing to take God's gift of salvation and give nothing back to Him."

Alan nodded his head. "That's your boy," he said. "Motivation for a lot of things, I have. But motivation for God or His service," —he threw his arms wide—"I scarcely know what the words mean. So fire away. I want to know what makes a fellow like you tick, and what gives you such a sense of fulfillment. And I want you to lay it on the line," he urged with an earnestness strange to him.

Peter did, and one day, sitting in the office Alan had blurted out, "Last night I told God I was available for whatever He wants. Now can you help me from there?"

During their subsequent conversations, Alan had told him about his life, that seemed to have taken him everywhere.

"I always had a yen to do something different," he had said on one of the occasions. "I've been scuba diving on the Florida Keys. I've gone spelunking in the caves of Virginia. I've been mountain climbing in British Columbia. I own my own plane and a glider. You name it, and if it's above or below sea level, I've done it. Now I'm nearly forty, and I just don't want to feed and gorge my ego any longer. I want to simplify and slim my soul," and he chuckled as he placed his hands on his ample hips. "These by the way nearly got me into trouble once, when I was spelunking, and got stuck in a cave about 300 feet underground. I had to make like a squirrel," and he scrabbled at imaginary earth with his hands, "and then I only got out because my pals wondered why I took so long catching up to them, and they came back looking for me."

"But I'm serious," he went on, "about slimming my soul. When I heard you talking about Africa and service for others, all that I have been doing seems shallow. It seems to me that love for others,—compassion, as you were saying—add some meaning to life. I must do something with whatever of life is left for me. So here I am, in your hands," he said as he waited for some miracle from his new friend.

Dunning was distressed. He knew that there must be something good in store for this man, yet it was not for him to direct a life. He let the silence envelop them again. Then he spoke:

"Alan, I don't have any magic formula for you. You tell me that you are a Christian, that your brokerage business gives you plenty of money and free time, that you can fly, dive and burrow," and the other man's head came up, the irrepressible grin crossing his face. "Let me just ask you one question. *Can you kneel?*"

The head of the other man swiveled around until they were looking at each other, eye to eye, as only honest men can do. Peter did not need to amplify. He just held the eyes of the other man in a silent stare, until the other's broke before him, and then the man nodded mutely.

"*Touché*," and he flicked his fingers from his lips in a gallic kiss. "I needed that, and the answer is no. At least I haven't tried kneeling yet. I sort of thought I could work things out myself, with a little assist from you," he added.

Dunning waited for a minute, then went on. "Some years ago, I was trying to plan my life, and everything seemed to fall apart. Then a good friend of mine, a high school teacher, taught me that *he only conquers who kneels*. It's the Cromwellian 'fight on your knees, but keep your powder dry' type of thing. You don't have to throw overboard everything you are and have. It all gets sublimated to the will of God when you learn to kneel in humility and submission." He paused. "Sorry, I didn't mean to start preaching. I just want you to know that I am the best listening post in Toronto, and am here whenever you want or need me. But the only help I can give is this counsel: get on your knees and get all your life straightened out before God. Set up a trysting place with Him and you'll find yourself flying higher than you have ever dreamed possible. Remember this?" and he flipped open a Bible and took out a piece of paper that had been creased and recreased.

"I'm no flyer myself," he said, "but there is an experience with God that lifts you up above the ordinary and commonplace. Gives you wings, so to speak. Anyway, listen to this poem by John Gillespie Magee that you heard the other day. He was a man after your own heart. He began: "Oh I've slipped the surly bonds of earth' and continued on until he came to the last three lines. Then with muted tone, he quoted;

> 'And, while with silent, lifting mind I've trod,
> The high untrespassed sanctity of space,
> *Put out my hand, and touched the face of God.*' "

There was silence in the room for a moment. Then Alan, who had listened as though hearing it for the first time, let his breath out as though he had been holding it in. "That's my boy," he said, "he wrote just what I have felt a hundred times, but

couldn't say. 'Put out my hand and touched the face of God,' "
he quoted.

Dunning waited, then quietly he said, "You don't touch the face
of God in a plane, Alan. You touch Him on your knees. Learn to
kneel, if you really want to go higher."

Once again there was silence. Then Peter went on: "Take a
couple of days, a week or a couple of weeks. Then come back to
me and we will talk. By then you may not only be off the merry-
go-round, but have the brass ring in your hand as well."

The two men stood up. Their hands met across the desk, and
Alan turned to leave, walking as Peter noticed before, with a
peculiar, loose kneed stride. Then he was gone, and Dunning
turned to the work on his desk.

# VI

He was leaving his office, and turned to switch off the light, when he felt, rather than heard someone standing in the shadow outside. Taking his hand from the light switch, he called out: "Who is there?"

There was the sound of movement, then someone slowly entered the office. It was Max Wald, one of the senior students, who had been in to see him several times during the past year. Dunning liked Max and had enjoyed his friendship in a way that was unusual between student and teacher. Perhaps the fact he was older than most students and was married, accounted for the familiarity.

Wald was somewhere over thirty, with a dark, almost swarthy complexion enhanced by his farm life and long hours spent in the sun. He was of middle height, slim, with the controlled grace of a man in excellent physical condition. His jet black hair framed a broad, clear forehead. Just now as he entered the office there was a look of uncertainty, almost discontent on his face.

"You were leaving, sir?" he asked in that deferential tone that seemed to be such a part of the man.

"I was," replied the other, "but not if you want something."

The visitor lowered himself into a chair, folded his strong, tanned hands across his lap, and sat there looking at them. He raised his eyes, and Dunning saw a look of distress in their depths. He waited.

"I've been walking around wondering whether to come in and talk to you or try to reason the thing out by myself," he said, almost abruptly. "You know that I will be graduating in a couple of weeks, and it seems that I am at a crossroads as far as making a decision about my future."

Peter waited. The man needed a listening post, and he was ready to provide it. After a pause he went on: "I have talked it over with Dorothea, and she thought that I should come and let you at least know what is happening. You don't know," he said, flashing a crooked grin, "what a fortunate man I am to have a wife like Dorothea. I just wish I had her faith and confidence," and he sighed. "And she has the three children to think of too. Well, here goes." He took a deep breath as though to take a plunge into cold water, and began.

"My grandfather used to say to me, 'Max, I don't want you to be one of those who has to stand up twice to make a shadow.'

"I thought it was sort of an old man's humor. Now I think I know what he meant. 'Make something of your life, and make it good. Don't keep on doing shadowless things'. Whatever he meant, I know that I don't want to have to stand up twice to make a shadow. I want to do the right thing with my life.

"Anyway, I've been wondering about the next steps after Bible College, and there are several things that I have to thrash out before I can take them." He spread out his hands as if laying them all on the desk between them.

Dunning tapped his teeth with the carved ebony letter opener that always seemed to be in his hands when he sat at the desk. The fingers of one hand went through his thinning, fair hair in a nervous gesture. He always felt something tighten up within him when he was counseling like this. Afraid of putting undue influence on the counselee, he was likewise afraid of not being emphatic enough.

*The Holy Spirit has to do the work,* he had thought often. *But where does the human element come in?* Then he would just give himself to listening, and often in that setting, the answer or decision was most evident. With a quiet prayer for the man now sitting in front of him, he waited.

"The two big issues right now," went on Max, "are my family

. . . my father and mother I mean . . . and my denomination. I know that Mother and Dad won't stand in the way of anything I feel God wants me to do. But I am the last son at home and Dad was hoping to turn over his farm to me to carry on. It's an excellent farm," he went on, "I might even say prosperous.

"Well, I haven't told them yet that I have been thinking seriously about the mission field, although they do know that I will most likely give up farming and do some kind of Christian work. In fact my mother said to me the other day 'Max, there are others who can work farms or serve at home. Not many will go to the mission field.' Anyway, I will have to decide soon. My church wants me to take over a charge at home here, and it looks most inviting." He waited again for a moment. "I have a wife and three children. I'm over thirty and whatever I decide I will have to start soon.

"I still can't get away from that call to Africa I told you about. But how do you *know* the right thing to do?" and he looked hopefully at his teacher-friend.

Dunning leaned forward. "I have no ready answer, Max," he said gently, "but I do know that there are several steps that you can take that will help you to find it. If you really want to know which way God would have you to go, that is," he added.

"Mr. Dunning, I wouldn't be here at the college in the first place, or talking to you now in the second place, if I wasn't completely sincere and honest," he caught himself. "Sorry, sir," his wide mouth split into a shamefaced grin, "I've just been living with the problem for so long and feel it so much that I guess I'm touchy. I really want to know God's will for my life," he answered the question, looking straight into the eyes of the older man, "and I'm ready to do anything necessary to do it," and he settled back in his chair.

Dunning tapped his teeth again, as though seeking the right words to say. "There are two things I want you to do," he said, finally, "and when you have done these, come back and we will talk."

"First, this is not just your decision. Your wife and family are involved in it too. Go home and have a good talk with Dorothea, making sure that you are both of the same mind. Then have a talk with your parents and let them know what you are thinking about. Remember, this will mean giving up the security that the farm holds for you and your family.

"Then set a time when you and Dorothea will pray, and pray definitely that you will make the right decision. The Lord will help you to plan as you should. He will bring something to your attention through reading or counseling. Somehow He will break through and you will know definitely 'this is the way; walk ye in it.'

"Take a couple of weeks, Max, and then come back and see me. I'm confident that you will have the answer or at least an inkling of what you should do."

"Thanks," said Max getting to his feet. "I know that Dorothea is with me in this, but it helps to talk it out with someone else you know."

"Counseling with Christian friends is good," conceded Peter, "but when the individual deals with the Lord, and through prayer and Bible reading is spiritually prepared, I'm convinced that he will receive the best of counseling from the Holy Spirit Himself."

"I'll be back in a week or two then," said Max. "Pray about my father. I know that this will be a big disappointment to him."

"I'll do that," said Peter, giving his hand that extra pressure of friendship. The response was firm, and Max turned and left the office.

It was less than a week later, that the two men found themselves in the same positions on either side of the desk.

"You have your answer," said Peter somewhat abruptly.

"Partly," replied the other. "How did you know?"

"Sixth sense, I guess. But there is a change in your appearance and attitude, and you don't look as harried and worried as you did before. This only comes with peace of mind and heart."

"You're right." replied Max. "Dorothea and I are both convinced that it must be Africa, and we have already written to our denominational mission board regarding it. Mother and Dad were wonderful," he burst out, a slight sign of tears in his eyes.

"Most parents are," replied Peter smiling.

"Dad is going to sell the farm, and I will have a share in the profits which should be of real help to get started on this missions bit. By the way," he added, "I want to tell you that it was when Dorothea and I began to pray very definitely about the future, and showed our willingness to take the steps that we would have to take, that things began to fall into place. Everything we did seemed to be the most natural in the world. Even our children noticed the difference, and they are now thrilled at the prospect of Africa. I confess that I am too, although I expect that it will be hard going. Good thing I'm used to hard work," and he flexed his strong, brown hands.

The two men sat talking for a long time. To Peter it seemed as though he had expected this answer all the time, and he was full of information about the land to which Max would be going.

"Tell you what," he said finally. "Why don't you and Dorothea come up and see Ruth and me sometime soon. The women can have a field day talking about what is needed out there, and we can give you a fairly good picture of what you will expect."

"That will be wonderful," exclaimed Max. "I'll speak to Dorothea about it. By the way," and he pulled a sheet of paper from his inner pocket, "last night I couldn't sleep, and I got out of bed and wrote this. This morning I showed it to Dorothea, and we both signed it. I'm giving it to you as the witness to our 'deed,'" and he handed Peter the paper, turned and left hurriedly.

Dunning looked down at the paper in his hand. He read:

"Our Dedication: During the past few weeks we have learned the necessity of staying close to Christ and of knowing His guiding hand regarding our life service for Him. Foreign missions was always meant for someone else, but not for us. Now we are giving the Lord a chance to use us wherever He wishes in this world of His.

"It is our sole purpose to remain faithful unto death to the One who conquered death for us. We have yet a lot to learn, and a lot of areas to perfect for our Lord, but by the help of God we trust that we shall be "more than conquerors through Christ.' "*

Peter felt a lump in his throat. This was the expression of a man who had met God in a new way. "Faithful unto death," repeated Peter, of the words that had arrested his attention. "May he prove so to be."

* These are a few of the sentences taken from the handwritten testimony of Merlin Grove, martyred in Somalia, in 1962. It was found in his file at Toronto Bible College after his death.

# VII

It was exactly two weeks later, that Peter heard a tap on his door, and saw the grinning face of Alan Volkes. As Alan saw another man sitting in the chair that he had previously occupied, he muttered a hurried "excuse me."

"Alan, wait," called out Dunning, and motioned him in. "I want you to meet a friend of mine. Max Wald, meet Alan Volkes. With two German names like that you should be friends." Their hand clasp was hurried, then both sat down.

"Max has just come to see me about his future work," Dunning began, "I've been talking to him for several weeks now, and it seems to me he is taking about the same course that you are. He wants to get off the merry-go-round," and he smiled as he saw the grin break over the older man's face, "and you have both been following the same prescription. I thought it would be good to talk together," and he settled back in his chair.

Somewhat diffidently, Alan looked down at his hands, then taking in both men, he said: "Well, I don't know if I'm off the merry-go-round, but I'm in a peculiar position if I'm not." Wrinkles appeared around his eyes and the corners of his mouth. "Ever try kneeling on a merry-go-round?" and he looked first at Dunning then at Wald. "For the first time in my life I have really tried to take stock of myself, and I found that all I could do was to get down on my knees and give myself over again to the Lord Jesus Christ.

"It works, Peter," he went on, "now I'm here the next lesson."

Wald looked at him, the worried lines on his face relaxing at the free and easy manner of this newcomer.

"Mr. Dunning and I have been talking about the very same thing," he said at last, his voice soft and quiet. "It was just last week that I finally turned everything I have over to the Lord, to do with whatever He wills."

"Max here, is in a little different situation than you, Alan," said Dunning. "He is married, has three children, a prosperous farm, and he's thirty-two years of age. Why should a fellow want to change a pattern like that, with everything going for him? Well, all I know is that God's ways are past finding out, and you have both done just what was needed to be done: learned to kneel, submit and obey. Max is most likely going to Africa," he added.

"Hey!" the ejaculation came from Alan. "That's my ticket—at least I both think and hope so," and he looked at Peter.

The latter just spread his hands out in a non-committal gesture. Inside, he felt a great glow, but he merely smiled.

"If I can use my training . . . or do we talk about that?" Alan added.

"We talk about it all right," said Peter, suddenly chuckling. "I was just wondering where a tribe of cave dwellers might be living. A spelunking missionary would be something different in this day of high specialization," and the three of them laughed. "Seriously though, these things should be taken into account, but not allowed to frame the decisions about where to go and what to do. Max is a farmer, and agricultural missionaries are desperately needed. Maybe Max is to be one. Maybe not. You are a pilot. This may be what God wants, but He also may want you to slog it out on foot. I don't know, and I have no answers, but there are some things that we can do."

For the next hour the three men talked together. For Dunning it was a case of directing the conversation only. He knew how easily his own ideas could grip these men and he hesitated to step on to what he thought was holy ground. *This is God's prerogative*, he thought to himself. *He must lead them on.*

When the hour was up the men got to their feet. "Still kneeling?" queried Peter. As the men both nodded, he went on. "The thing to do now is just to leave yourself wide open. Something you hear or see or that comes to your attention, or something that the Lord puts into your mind will be the key that will open the door. Then you can start going through it."

Before they left he put his arms around both the men, and quietly prayed for them and for the unknown future. Then another handshake and they were gone.

Dunning turned back to his desk with the day's mail still lying in its neat pile before him. He busied himself, sorting it out, first class mail for immediate attention, second class and periodicals for later perusal. He rifled through the first class letters. Suddenly he dropped the others, and slit open one that bore a Nigerian stamp. *My old field,* he thought, as he pulled the lightweight paper out of the airmail envelope. The old familiar longing and nostalgia beginning to build up in him again.

It was a general news letter from his old friend Raymond Dawes, a mission executive. Peter settled back and read the two typed pages.

He set it down and whistled. Then checked himself. *I'm glad I didn't read this before Alan came,* he muttered to himself. *I would most likely have used it as a lever.* He re-read the letter:

"If we don't get another qualified pilot soon we cannot risk putting our planes in the air," he read. "The two men we have are so exhausted that it would be dangerous to have them do much more jungle flying. One of them is overdue for furlough, and our air arm is desperately needed right now.

"Our school program that we have been longing and praying for now seems ready to launch. We only lack teachers. If there are any men or women who qualify for any of this work, could you let them know of the opportunity?"

Dunning sat back. "Easy does it," he said to himself, "God doesn't need an assist along the way. I'll hold this until I see what happens." He slipped the letter into a file basket, and turned to the rest of his mail.

# VIII

Alan Volkes and Bill McAdams stood beside the Piper Pacer in the African jungle clearing. Nearby, Baru held the reins of the two frightened horses.

"Now about that breakfast," Alan looked at the other man.

"What about the plane, will it be all right?" asked Bill.

"I'd prefer to have someone look after it. Do you think Baru would?" and he nodded in the direction of the African.

"I'll ask him," and suiting his words, Bill went to his friend and spoke to him.

"Baru, would you let the pilot ('*Mai jirgin sama*' he called him) ride your horse back to the Mission? If you will stay here and guard the plane, I'll send someone back with the horses and he can bring you some food."

"*To, Likita* (all right Doctor)" replied Baru, "I am not as you, eating three meals a day," and he chuckled and touched his lean midriff, "and I will be glad to stay and guard this big dragon fly," and he indicated the plane.

Bill returned to the pilot. "A.O.K.," he grinned as he used the space age jargon that seemed so out of place here in the African bush. "He says he will stay if he doesn't have to drive it," he interpreted for his friend, "and I assured him that he just had to keep monkeys and people away from it, and that I would send him a horse and some food. He and the others will guard it until you are ready to go."

"Good show," replied Alan. Going back to the plane, he reached behind the seat of the cockpit, pulled out a flight bag,

47

and four great wooden blocks joined in pairs by heavy springs.

Carefully closing the cockpit door, he twisted the handle up, and Bill heard the sharp click as it locked in place. Then Alan carefully placed two blocks under each wheel and locked them tightly against the tires. Picking up the small bag, and with his peculiar walk, he came back to the missionary and the horses.

"As I said, with my luck it will be a horse," he said in mock horror as he approached. "Which end do I get on and how do you steer the thing?"

"You get on in the middle," and Bill chuckled at the humor.

He took the pilot's flight bag, and fastened it behind his own saddle by the special straps that he had contrived for carrying a medical kit. "Need any help to mount?"

"Not me," said the other. "Horse or plane, I'll do it on my own." So saying he approached the horse, whose reins Baru surrendered to him, put his foot in the stirrup, and the next minute was hopping down the road like some giant bird, one foot cocked up and under the horse's belly, the other vainly seeking to stop his relentless march back down the road.

Baru ran after him, muttering something in his own tongue that Bill could not catch, caught the horse's reins near the bit and waited while the pilot extricated his foot.

"Now try the other side," chided Bill. "You mount a horse on the left, just like getting into a plane," he couldn't resist adding. "And it might be wise to let Baru give you a leg up." He said something in Hausa, saw Baru hold his hand near his knee and invite the man to step into it, then swing his free leg over the horse's back. Baru then placed the pilot's feet carefully in the stirrups, sensing that his doctor friend was bantering the pilot, while Alan docilely permitted him to do the job.

With the skill of long practice, Bill swung into his saddle, and putting his horse alongside the other, he said: "She will follow mine. We'll take it slowly until you get used to the motion," and he dug his heels into the horse's flank, and moved off down the road.

The two men rode on in silence, the quiet of the bush broken only by the soft pad of the horses' hooves. The pace was slower than Bill liked and he had to hold his horse in with a strong hand to keep close to his friend.

"Little bit different from flying?" he asked the question, turning in his saddle to do so. The look of concentration on the face of the pilot made him chuckle. The man's head came up on hearing the question, and he saw the grin on the face of McAdams.

"The comparison is odious," he replied, "and from the smell of this horse, I mean odious," and his face creased in a grin. "I'm concentrating on *not* flying at this moment . . . flying over his head I mean," and he gripped the saddle horn a little more firmly. "Give me a plane any day to this," and he grimaced as the horse stumbled slightly on the uneven roadway.

"Just another five miles," said Bill cheerfully to the groans of the other. "If you want to get there sooner we could travel a little faster," he suggested hopefully.

"You mean let this horse go faster with me on it?" and he shook his head. "I'm having enough trouble now. O.K., let's shake them up a bit . . . me I mean. And I'll try to fly her straight."

Bill clucked to his horse, touched her lightly with his heels, shook the reins loosely on her neck, and felt her gather for that spine tingling gallop that they both loved. He looked back as he did so.

Alan Volkes was unprepared for the sudden bolt of the horse he was riding and only his death clutch on the pommel saved him from falling. As Bill's horse, with a little whinny of delight, settled into its long-legged gallop, the other horse followed. The first few strides felt ungainly, uncomfortable and dangerous to the amateur rider. Then suddenly the pace smoothed out, he found himself rising fairly easily in his saddle to compensate for the up and down motion of the horse's back, and for the first time he felt something of the exhilaration of riding.

Bill looked back, and smiled. The man behind him at first resembled nothing less than a giant heron, its wings flapping violently as it strove to get its ungainly body into the air. His elbows were flapping at his side. His knees seemed to be akimbo instead of hugging the horse for proper balance. His head joggled helplessly on his neck. *Ichabod Crane,* thought Bill, as he remembered the description of that hapless lover from Sleepy Hollow. *Ichabod Crane rides again,* and he turned back to the joy of his own mount.

When he looked back next Alan had settled into the saddle and seemed less ungainly. On his face was a look of pure joy, the initiation of the tenderfoot into the thrill of horseback riding.

*Wait until he gets off,* thought Bill to himself. *Then he will know that he's been riding.*

The rapid pace now brought them closer to the compound gate which was still open, and gathered around it was the usual crowd of Africans who had heard the horses coming with that acute hearing that had been bred into the children of the jungle. The horses, now sensing their stable and the fodder that would await them came through the gate, bushy tailed and high stepping, and once again the look of consternation spread over Alan's face.

Then he saw Jane standing near the center of the compound, her hand shading her eyes. Trying to be nonchalant, he released his hold on the pommel, sat up straight, and suddenly found himself with his face buried in the long mane of the horse. His arms went convulsively around its neck and his last few yards were ignominious. The horse stopped suddenly, checked by the strong hand of one of Baru's sons, and Alan's mouth was filled with horse hair. He sputtered, slowly sat up straight to see the laughing face of Jane peering up at him.

"Oh, hello," said Alan, still pulling horse hair from his mouth. "I must have been asleep. So restful up here," and he looked down with his infectious grin.

The girl laughed, and waited as her husband, now dismounted, came over to them. "O.K., Alan?" he asked anxiously. "Was that too fast for you?"

"Wasn't fast enough if you know what I mean," replied the other. "How do you get down off this ruddy thing?"

"Just turn around and slide off over its tail," suggested Bill. "It's easy when you know how."

Alan looked at him in disbelief. "Look, I've seen enough crummy westerns on television, and bad as they are, they at least show how to get on and off horses properly."

"Mount and dismount are the proper terms," said Bill, solicitously. "One must learn the proper terms."

Again Alan looked at Bill, but the doctor's face was straight and showed only concern. "Look," said the latter, "perhaps we could have a little discussion as to the merits of dismounting over the tail, over the head, or on either side. What do you think, Jane?" and he turned to his wife who fell into the mood.

"We could get some of the other men to come. Oh no, I have a book on horsemanship. I'm sure the best methods would be in that," and she turned towards the house.

"Come back here," the roar from Alan made the horse side step nervously, and once more he was gripping the pommel. "Sorry, ma'am," he tipped the baseball cap to her, "begging your pardon, ma'am, I think that a cold drink, some light refreshment and a soft pillow," and he grimaced as he shifted his position in the saddle, "are called for. I want to get down off this beast," he moaned piteously.

"Oh, why didn't you say so?" Jane was still teasing him. "I'll get some of the children here to help you down," and turning she called to a group of African children, who came close to the horse, and looked up at the rider in mischievous glee.

At another word from Jane, they stretched up their little arms toward the rider, while Jane said: "There, now you are safe, and can jump into their arms."

At that Alan threw up both hands. The horse, startled by the sudden movement moved forward. His hands up in the air, the rider had no means of support, one foot came out of the stirrup in a convulsive thrust back, the other followed, as with dexterity that belied his ignorance of dismounting, he whirled sideways, bounced lightly on his feet, and was bowing before Jane, with his cap in his hand all in a grand sweeping gesture.

"Your servant, Alan Volkes, ma'am," and he looked up at her with his wide grin.

Bill joined them. "I guess introductions are useless after that," and he placed an arm around his wife, and laid the other on the shoulder of their new friend.

Jane put out her hand. "What a welcome to give a stranger," she said, "but somehow I think you asked for it."

"And got more than I asked for," he replied, taking the hand she offered him. "But I feel at home already. Although at home, I usually have breakfast. . . ." and he left the sentence trailing.

With a chuckle Jane turned towards the house to get the breakfast ready while the two men followed.

# IX

With breakfast over, the three sat with the dirty dishes in front of them as Alan talked.

He told them of his own life, understating the heroics and adventure that the other two felt lurked under the surface, and finally came to what they had been wanting to hear.

"Your friend Peter Dunning is quite a guy," he began, then told them of the banquet and subsequent talks with their friend, and his ultimate decision to come to Africa as a missionary pilot. He told of his strong conviction that he could use his training in this way, a conviction confirmed when Peter told him of the desperate need for a pilot-mechanic "for which the R.C.A.F. prepared me," he added with a chuckle.

"I've been out for three months now," he added, "and this is my first flight out your way. I really wondered if I would be able to land at all," and he waved his hand towards the jungle that surrounded the mission compound.

"So Dunning used to live here," he added, and he looked around curiously as though trying to see the man in this environment.

"Well, not in this house," said Bill. "I had this built for Jane. Peter and Ruth had a house over at the far end of the compound," and he thrust forth his chin in the general direction, in the expressive way of the African. Pointing with the finger or hand could be interpreted as a curse, and he had long since adopted this method of showing direction. "We use their place as a guest house, at least until they come back. Are they coming?" and Alan heard the underlying anxiety in the voice.

"Doesn't look like it for awhile," he said. "Seems he is still having some trouble from that cerebral malaria. But if there ever was a man who lives for Africa, it's Peter Dunning," and he nodded his head decisively.

He saw the disappointment in their faces, then went on: "But he sent a message for you. I'll have to put it into my own words, since he said that he wouldn't write it, although I did make him write down a few words that I didn't understand or couldn't remember."

He opened the flap of a pocket on his bush jacket and pulled out a small pink slip. As he unfolded it, Bill saw the words: 'Memo From the Desk of Peter Dunning' across the top of it. Then below were a few words written, indecipherable from where he was sitting.

"He said first of all to give you his . . . is the word *kauna*? . . . his *kauna*, whatever that is."

"It's the Hausa word for love," said Bill, "the strongest word in fact. The other word could be translated 'like.' This is love in its fullest sense. I know what he means."

"Well, he sends you his love, and wants you to share it with Baru, and someone else . . . is there a Chuna?" When Bill and Jane had nodded, he went on, "and you are to greet all the others here who remember him.

"That was just the first part of the message. His next one is, he wondered what you thought of the possibility of flying into the . . . Kitta tribe?" he raised his voice and eyebrows, "the Kitta tribe where you and he had been planning to open up a work. He said he thought that we might be able to land on a sandy bank of the river down there during the dry season when the water is not very high. He thought that we might be able to go down there sometime and look it over from the air, then try to get permission to land."

Bill was sitting forward, his hands tucked under his arm pits, as he listened. "Just the thing," he exclaimed. "We've been wanting to get down that way for years but never did get beyond the place the people called the Tangled Mountain. Remember that Jane?" and he turned to his wife.

"Can I ever forget it," she almost whispered it. In her mind was the picture of the days of uncertainty that had nearly cost their nurse co-worker, Pat Donnell, her life.* The memory was so vivid that she shivered.

"Well," went on the visitor, "that's another item. By the way he called that Mountain Bima, according to the notes here. Same difference?" and when Bill nodded, he went on.

"Then he thought that you would like to know that Pat Donnell is getting around with the help of two canes now, and there is every hope that she may be left with just a slight limp from her attack of polio. It was here she got it, wasn't it?" he asked.

"Right here," Jane answered for them. "And I'll never forget how I prayed for Bill to get back here from the Tangled Mountain, or how the Wigle's iron lung saved her life."

"Yeah, Peter told me about that," said Alan. "I met Pat, too. He wanted me to tell you that Pat and Mike hope to be married sometime in July." Jane uttered a squeal of pleasure, and Bill grinned. "They're a great pair. Sometime I'll tell you about them. Their lives have been a real challenge to those of us who knew them."

Jane was more explicit. "They're the kind of people that I think Christians should really be," she said pertly. "I honestly don't know if I would have the faith to have done what they did. They wanted God's will. They did it because of their deep love and dedication to Christ. I don't know . . . sometimes I wonder if I would face up to a real test to my faith. When Mike couldn't come to the field because of a growth in his lung they felt that Pat should come anyway. I don't know if I could have done it," and she looked at her husband.

"When the time comes you'll know," said Bill, little dreaming that it would soon be there and that they would both have to face

* As told in *Beyond the Tangled Mountain* by the same author.

it. "It's hard to say what you will do until the time comes and you are confronted with a decision." He turned back to Alan.

"There must be something else that Peter said," and he looked at the man. "All this he could have sent us in a letter. What message did he really give you?"

Volkes reached into the pocket of his bush jacket again, and pulled out a sealed letter. "Well," he drawled slowly, "he did say that I had to deliver this to you personally. I think he just wanted an excuse to get me to come in here and meet you," he added almost apologetically. "Here is what he calls my letter of introduction," and he handed it to Jane.

She took it eagerly and with Bill hitching his chair closer so that they could read it together, she scanned the first of several pages of the familiar handwriting of their closest friend.

"Dear Bill & Jane," they read. "When you are reading this you will be sitting somewhere near one of the finest men that I have met in a long time. I told him that he must deliver this message to you personally, so I know that he is nearby.

"Take a good look at him," and Alan, watching them saw them both look at him over the letter, and hastily looked away. "There sits a man who has *put out his hand and touched the face of God*.

"I met him in a way that he can tell you about, but when I enquired about him, I could scarcely believe that all that he has done was done by one man.

"He most likely won't tell you everything, although if you can start him yarning you will get some idea of where he has been and what he has done. If it is above or below earth, he has done it. He's one of those restless, able men who, in any century would have been an adventurer, explorer or what have you. Somewhere along the line he found he was fed up with having done everything and accomplished nothing, and seemed at loose ends. The Lord brought us together and it has been my privilege to help him.

"He had an accident that nearly cost him his sight, if not his life, and it got him thinking about life and its purpose. Well, he can tell you how it all happened, but one day while we were talking, he said that he wondered if 'my Africa' would ever want a broken-down pilot. Broken down! I know for a fact that he is one of the most able men at the local flying club. The others there speak of him almost with awe. I think his only real regret in life is that he was not able to fly during the war. The R.C.A.F. missed one of the best . . . but I think it was all in God's plan. He can take a plane apart and put it together almost blindfolded, and one of his friends told me that if he put wings on an orange crate he could make it fly.

"Anyway, he seemed the real type for the jungle flying that is necessary if our job is ever going to get done in Africa, and we talked and prayed about it, until . . . well, there he is. I had so little to do with it, it would almost seem funny, if I didn't know how God works.

"There he is then, a good friend of mine sitting with the best friends God ever gave to a man. You know the love I have for you and Jane. Take Alan in, see if what I say about him is true, and perhaps he will do what I cannot do right now . . . get down to that south area with a small plane *and reach that southern Kitta tribe for Christ.*

"Receive him as a brother in the Lord. I will wait for word about your meeting, and what might be planned for the future.

God bless you both . . . you three,

Peter and Ruth."

Jane folded the letter up and returned it to its envelope. She and Bill looked at each other and they saw the same thing in each others' eyes.

"Welcome to the club," and they both put hands out to their visitor. "The club of Peter Dunning's admirers," added Jane. "We think he is about the best. You got to know him pretty well?" she continued as she withdrew her hand.

"I think so," replied Alan. "He got to know me pretty well, anyway. He is one of the few men that I have been able to talk to freely and easily, and I guess he served as a sort of father confessor," and the man grinned, almost shyly.

"Guess we all feel that way about him," said Bill. "But as we say, welcome to the club."

Little did Bill know that Alan would be the means of saving lives and nearly losing his own. Now there was laughter. Then there were to be tears and fears. The future was blessedly hidden from them all.

# X

"Tell me about this Kitta tribe," Alan asked eagerly. Bill McAdams quickly briefed him, while Jane listened quietly.

Peter Dunning and Bill McAdams had heard of the Kitta people for years. The stories of their fierce, proud warriors were legion. Baru had often told them of this inaccessible, primitive tribe, and how he himself longed to seek to enter there and preach Christ to them.

"Since Christ has come to our people, much darkness has gone," Baru had said on one occasion, as he and the doctor sat talking together. "What the gospel has done for us, it can do for them, no matter how much *tsafi* (witchcraft) they believe in."

"But it is impossible to get into the place where they live," Bill added as Alan listened intently. "They live near a river south of us here, but between us and the river is an almost impassible jungle: And some who have tried to get through have never returned. We thought perhaps if we could come in by the river, and show them that we are people of peace, they might listen to us."

The missionaries had thus salted 'project Kitta' away to wait for some opportune time when they might be able to take the long, round-about trip that would bring them to the river, and perhaps travel by dugout canoe to the Kitta villages. It was one of those dreams that missionaries all over the world seem to have: a needy people in an inaccessible area, all but lost to the twentieth century, and still living as they did in the stone age. Like a whiff of foul air, like the miasma of some fetid swamp

59

hole, stories came out of these fastnesses that made the blood curdle.

Murder and bloodshed, head hunting and witchcraft, darkness and terrorism . . . these chilled the most hardened of adventurous spirits.

The Kittas were without either modern weapon or tools. To fight or to hunt they used long lances, great six foot, hardwood spears with needle point tips, that they threw with incredible accuracy. Bows and arrows were also used, and for close killing, knives were carried in a sheath strapped to the forearm.

So great is their fear or hatred of strangers they have been known to kill and eat even a stray dog that ventured into their area. And it was to such a place that Dunning and McAdams had been longing to go for nearly five years. But Christian missions is not a game, it is not a pleasant hobby or past-time. It is a warfare that demands stamina and sacrifice. It is deadly, earnest, a struggle against the powers of darkness.

Like warfare, it could mean casualties, and it did demand planning and preparation. McAdams knew that when the time was ripe there would be a way in and a work done for God. In the meantime there was prayer and preparation.

And now there was a man and his little plane. Could this be the time?

Bill McAdams looked at the man before him seeking to grasp what this could mean. Had Dunning, with prophetic foresight, seen what could be done? For a moment his heart quailed, then was calm. God's time is always the right time.

They had been talking about the letter from Dunning, and Bill finished briefing the pilot about the Kitta people.

"I just want to know one thing," said Alan. "Is there any place near there where we can set the plane down? Or better still, how about taking a run down there sometime and looking it over? You say there is a river. Is there a good bank or beach alongside it?" and as Bill shook his head disclaiming knowledge, the other went on, "Well, a good look at it should tell us both the possibility of landing and where their villages are." He stopped as Bill got up from the table and went to the door. They heard his stentorian 'Baru' and waited until they saw the African come into the house.

McAdams and his African friend came back to the table and they both sat down.

"I'm going to tell Baru what Peter has said, and perhaps he has some ideas about the place," said Bill by way of explanation, then he turned and in rapid Hausa told him what they had been talking about.

Baru nodded his head from time to time, his agile mind taking in this new possibility, and as he did so, his face creased in a great, wide grin.

"My friend," he replied to Bill, "I don't know anything about the canoe that flies (**jirgin sama**), but having seen what the stranger has done with his machine, I would think that he could land somewhere beside the river during the dry season when the water is low. I have never been down the river, but our people say that during the season when the rains have gone there are great stretches of land that is white, where the jungle cannot grow." *Sand*! thought Bill to himself.

He paused while Bill translated the conversation to the pilot. "Sounds like what you are hoping for," he added as the other nodded his head.

"As long as there is a clear stretch without logs or driftwood on it we should be able to land there," he replied, rubbing his hands with satisfaction. "You've seen how I can land on your road, and it can't be much worse than that!"

The four of them continued talking until a clanging bell broke into their conversation.

"Sorry," said Bill rising, "but I have a clinic this morning and there is quite a line of patients waiting for me. You sit here and talk and I'll get back as soon as I can."

"I'd rather watch you at the hospital," said Alan rising. "Not that I don't appreciate fair company," and he grinned at Jane, "but I want to see how you people operate out here . . . I use that word loosely," he said laughing, "since I am not in the least bit interested in watching you operate. I've experienced enough of that," and his eyes clouded for a moment as he recalled his own plane crash and subsequent hospital care. "But I want to see what makes a medical missionary tick," and waving to Jane, he followed the doctor out of the house.

"I didn't want to ask you in front of Jane, but is there any danger trying to get to the Kitta people?" he asked as they strode across the compound. "Or is she the worrying kind?"

"I guess she worries as much as most people would living out here like this," replied the other, "but so do I. But worry and wonder won't stop either one of us doing the job that we think God would have us to do. Jane is a brick, and she won't let anything or anyone stand in the way of the will of God. I only wish I could say the same for a lot of the people I met when I was on furlough," he added, kicking a stone out of the path with a skillful flick of his toe. "Too many people who profess to be Christians refuse to meet the challenge of the need and the lost condition of people outside of Christ. Too comfortable, I guess. I think I would have strangled if I had had to stay home after living out here for awhile. My heart bleeds for Peter," and he fell silent until they reached the small hospital.

They passed through the double line of patients, his eye darting here and there to note the various cases that had come. Men, women and children, of all ages, and all sizes, some well dressed, some in tatters, some standing, some squatting, some being supported by friends and relatives.

*And to think I once almost gave this up to help an effete society at home, with their imaginary ills, or their very real needs but pampered and served by a society that seemed to care only for self,* thought Bill to himself. He shuddered.

Bounding up the stairs he soon left the pilot behind, and indeed seemed oblivious to the visitor as he set about his work. His well-trained dispensers could care for many of the cases, but each one of them must have a visit from the white doctor (**bature mai magani**) and Bill knew that his day would be full.

With a sigh of satisfaction, he put out his hands towards the first patient that was allowed in. He was a tyke of a boy, with an abdomen so swelled that he seemed unable to walk and support the load. The doctor ran his hands over the bloated abdomen, noted the great, hooked umbilical hernia, felt the hard rock of an enlarged spleen, then gave a crisp order to the dispenser. The boy was hustled away, to go into one of the few empty beds in the small ward. He was one who would have the special care of the missionary doctor.

He loved children, and it broke his heart to see the abuse and carelessness of some parents with their offspring. *If we have any children* . . . the thought was broken as the next patient was presented. Shaking his head to drive away his thoughts, he concentrated on the work at hand.

# XI

During the next few months they saw a lot of Alan who seemed to drop in whenever he had occasion to fly in their general direction. When he buzzed the mission station Baru needed no instructions to saddle the horses and meet the pilot down the road.

Horse and pilot seemed to be on better terms, and Bill often remarked that he handled her almost as easily as his plane.

"Could be, could be," declaimed the other with a wave of the hand. "Horse, plane or woman . . . all they need is a strong hand at the control. Show 'em who's boss," and he ducked as Jane playfully doubled up her fist and threatened him.

"What you need is a woman at the helm," she retorted.

He replied with a quizzical look: "Show me a spelunking female missionary, and I'll be glad to hitch on to the same life line," and he chuckled.

One day when he had turned up unexpectedly, he said to Bill: "At last I talked the powers-that-be into it."

"Into what?" asked Jane as they sat in the screened porch listening to the night sounds of Africa.

Alan looked at Jane and then at Bill. "There's only one thing to be considered right now," he spoke as to a little child, "and I'll explain it to you. Bill and I have had 'project Kitta' on our minds for months, hoping that we could take a survey flight down along the river." He stopped as he saw the look on Jane's face. In a moment she recovered herself.

"Sorry," she said, looking at Bill, "just felt queer for a moment.

I've heard about the fierce Kitta people so much since I arrived here that I . . ."

"We're not going in unless it seems wise to do so," replied Bill reassuringly. "This is just an aerial survey so we can see what the place looks like. Then if we can land there and make a contact, we are going to do so. But it will take a lot of careful planning and praying. Now that we have the green light we can start anytime."

Jane said no more. Not for the world would she have said anything that would deter her husband in this work to which they had both dedicated their lives. She only knew that there were occasions such as this one when fear clutched at her heart, and only the knowledge that their times were in God's hands kept her from succumbing to the fear. She looked at the two men now engrossed with their plans for the first flight over the unknown territory. Soon she too was caught up in the plans and the three of them talked far into the night.

Alan was bubbling over with anticipation, and even as he talked, Jane realized something of the nature of the man himself, one who had never been content merely to live. He needed adventure as the lungs need air.

Now he was telling them of an addition that he had made to his little plane that would make it as efficient as a twin engine job. "I was never happy with one little motor, winging my way around this country," he said, "yet, I knew that a twin engine for such a plane was an engineering impossibility. So I contrived an alternate fuel system and a dual ignition. Now I have the closest thing to a twin engine plane possible. So you won't have to worry about us suddenly landing in the middle of a Kitta village," he said, putting his hand on Jane's arm. "I assure you that your husband will be as safe as it is humanly possible to be. And when we get out of that realm," he added, "God will have to take over." The two friends nodded.

"By the way," he added, "I also have a two-way radio communication system in the plane to install here. We are putting them in every mission station so we can have almost instant contact all over the field. Now the plane can be called in and be available in a matter of a few hours at the most . . . depending on where I am flying that is," he added. "One of these days I'm going to rig up an ambulance-type bed for it. Not much fun sitting up on a flight when you should be kept flat on your back.

"We are also asking each mission station to clear out a landing strip as close to the work as possible," he went on. "Think the people here will release enough land to do it?"

"I think so," replied Bill. "In fact Baru was asking me why we don't make a straight stretch of motor road near here, so that you don't have to ride that horse in every time you come. I think he is really worried about you," and he laughed at the rueful look on his friend's face.

"Tell him for me, that that is the best news I have heard in a long time."

When the three of them finally separated for the night, it had been settled that as soon as an air strip was ready near the station, and the radio communication set up, that they would make their first survey of the Kitta people. For the two men the day of high adventure could not come too soon. For the woman, she could only wait and pray.

# XII

"Bill," Jane's voice cut into his subconscious mind, and with an effort he pulled himself out of the *Time* magazine he was reading. It was about a month old, but he was fascinated not by the relevance of the news, but by the coverage and colorful descriptions that made news live. He looked over at his wife, who was sitting like a little girl with her hands folded between her knees, and leaning forward looking full into his face. "Bill," she repeated, when she saw that at last she had his attention, "that's the fourth time I've spoken to you, by the way," she added with a grin.

"You want something special?" he asked in a voice that tried to be indifferent and casual. His effort failed. Bill never ceased to wonder at this woman who had given up so much to be his wife and to be with him in his work, buried in the jungle, away from the piano that had been a part of her life, and from music that seemed to be her very soul. His look as well as his tone conveyed the love that seemed to shine brighter and brighter every day.

Jane heard the words, but at the tone her own eyes brightened perceptibly, and there was a slight huskiness in her voice as she went on:

"You are a doctor, aren't you?" and her question carried something of his tone in it.

With a negligent wave of his hand, he motioned to his framed diploma from the University of Toronto hanging over the small desk at the far end of the room. "Proof positive," he said, "and

I have some other identification if it is required." Suddenly he sat bolt upright. "Something wrong?" and he couldn't keep the anxiety out of his voice, despite the discipline that he had long since laid upon himself.

"Depends on what you mean by 'something' and 'wrong'," she replied quietly. "There is nothing wrong, but definitely something is happening."

Suddenly her face crumpled and her last words were lost in a half fearful, half happy sob, as she flung herself across the room and put her arms around her husband's neck.

"Bill, I just thought you would like to know that I am going to have a baby, and if you are half as happy as I am, you'll shout so loudly that you will wake up the whole village," and she hugged his head to her breast.

There was a heart stopping moment as Bill took in the news. He had lived within the cycle of birth and death for so many years, and at such close quarters, that he was sure that no news could surprise him. Yet this was his wife, and this was his baby. This was the result of their love that was deep, so rich. His arm went around this woman whom he loved so completely. He knew his own skill and training were at her side. He also knew, from the awful knowledge that comes only to the man so completely isolated from the usual medical facilities, that danger lurked in a way that she must never know. His arm tightened around the slim waist that would soon be thickening with the growth of the child within her, and he waited until he felt complete control.

"Jane," and love surrounded the name, "Jane, why didn't you tell me before?"

"Just wanted to make sure, my dear medico," she smiled, as his face upturned to her. "Now I am sure, and if you can accept the word of a wife, you should be a proud father sometime in July." And once more she buried his head in her breast in a compulsive grasp that hid the slight tinge of fear or wonder that crossed her face.

Bill slowly disengaged himself from her embrace, stood up

and pulled her up and to him. "Dear, dear Jane," his big hand went to her head, smoothed the hair back from her brow, and tilted her face back until their eyes met. "Dear Jane, I loved you before. . . . I love you more than ever now. Imagine, me a father!" and he thrust her away to strut before her in such exaggeration that she began to laugh and the tinge of fear died within her.

"So now we have to do some planning and preparation," she went on, "and I was thinking that the best thing I could do would be to write to Ruth Dunning, and she could order what I need, and Peter could ship it out to us."

"And what do you need except a goat skin to tie the baby on your back?" enquired Bill, his eyebrows shooting up high. "I can get Baru to skin a very nice goat for you, and his wife can tan it so that it will be soft and pliable. She will even be able to show you how to sling the baby on your back and cover its head with a calabash, so that when you are out on the farm hoeing or chopping wood it will be protected from the sun. And," he went on, ticking off the imaginary items on his fingers . . . then ducked as she swung wildly at his head with a small clenched fist.

He caught her hand in his own, then pulled her to him, and holding her close, whispered in her hair. "Oh, my darling," and the words from this man who so rarely showed emotion made shivers run up her spine, "you don't know how happy this makes me feel. I've helped a lot of babies into this world, but this one is going to be a gold plated special," and he hugged her closer still.

For the next hour or so they sat and chatted about the big and new event that was coming into their lives. They talked about what would be needed, what they would purchase in the country and what they would have to send for. Soon, it seemed as though this had always been part of their three years of married life instead of just a few hours. There was something new and rich in their relationship and the glow on Jane's face grew more and more radiant.

"I can't get over this miracle of new life," she said finally to her husband, laying her hand on her abdomen. "All these weeks while I have been wondering if it were true or not, I have felt more than ever like what the Bible calls the 'handmaid of the Lord.' I only hope," she added somewhat pensively, "that I will be that, and that our child will grow up to be a servant of the One we both love." She stopped, and once more a lovely glow suffused her cheek.

"Bill," she went on, "I know that we have seven months to wait, but . . . would you dedicate our baby to the Lord? Now?"

"Dearest Jane," once more he spoke quietly, submissively. The knowledge of impending fatherhood had scarcely taken hold of him, but looking at her he began to feel something of what motherhood meant to her. This was the fulfilling of God's plan and purpose, and as it comes perhaps only once to a man of feeling as he tries to assimilate the news that he is going to be a father, he felt the touch of the sacredness of what his wife was going through.

"Dearest Jane," he whispered again, then kneeling down beside her and putting his head in her lap, and with her own hand resting upon his bowed head, he prayed–they prayed–for the safety of the little unborn mite, even now just a tiny fetus, a miniscule replica of the being it someday should be. The prayer was for the baby, for the mother, and for the life that would eventually break upon this world. It was a prayer of humility and submission, of anticipation and delight.

When the muffled voice of her husband was stilled, Jane sat quietly feeling the sense of exaltation and joy welling up within.

"A trinity," she whispered to herself, her hand still on her husband's head. "How fitting, that mother, father and child, should thus bow before the Trinity of God, who 'loved us and gave Himself for us.' And from her own heart there came the unspoken "amen" to all that her husband had said.

Thus she sat and he knelt, as the tropical sun quickly dropped without its twilight, and the darkness wrapped around them with the suddenness of a thrown blanket. And still they sat and knelt.

# XIII

Bill and Jane looked at one another over the remains of their breakfast, with the look of complete contentment that had been their special feeling during these months of waiting for the birth of the baby. Jane was big with child, her small, once-slim body almost overbalanced by the weight of the baby within her.

Bill looked at his wife, and marvelled at the miracle of impending motherhood. Despite the heat and obvious discomfort of her condition, Jane looked calm and poised, her face alight, her eyes dark rimmed, were shining with a deep joy that Bill had seen so often in the faces of his patients.

*The miracle of birth seems to touch them all with unearthly glory,* thought Bill, almost saying "a touch of the divine." To him there was something awesome that he had noticed even the primitive Africans whom he cared for seemed to sense as the birth of a baby neared.

"Sometime this month?" his question needed no further elucidation. Jane nodded, adding "You're the doctor, you should know," and crinkling her nose up at him across the table.

"I may be the doctor, but I'm also the father," he reminded her, "and the dual role is a difficult one to fill. For instance, I should be charging my patient a suitable fee for services rendered. After all, not many mothers have a personal physician to attend them. How much is it worth?"

"I'll ask my husband," she replied. "Perhaps he has figured out just what it is worth." She raised her voice slightly. "Bill, I just had a request from my doctor for services rendered. Instead of putting a charge in, he suggested we give what we think his services are worth. Ever priced a baby?" she asked.

Bill shifted from the chair in which he had been sitting to another. "Well, if I have to pay what this is worth I'll be a pauper for the rest of my life. You tell that doctor that from now on he can have all I am and have. I'll work for him every day, and anything he asks, I'll do it without question. Think that will satisfy him?"

"Seems fair enough," said Jane, as she watched her husband slide back into the chair he had been sitting in before. "Doctor, my husband says that the baby is without price, and he will be your slave for life. Now if you can just manage to pass some of that slavery over to me, I could use it right handily. Particularly with these breakfast dishes," and she touched some gingerly.

"Yours to command, ma'am," said her husband, sliding once more into the husband's seat. "This day I will start paying my honest debts." He began gathering up the dishes when his wife's hand closed over his.

"Listen," she said, her head cocked on one side, "isn't that the plane?"

"It's Alan," whooped her husband, dishes forgotten as he headed for the door.

"Bill, your debt!" Jane's voice reached him as he opened the screen door. "Remember me?"

With a grin he came back to her, took her arm, and began adjusting his pace to hers, helping her out the door and down the short flight of steps. In the time it had taken them to reach the open compound, the plane was now in sight, dropping lower as it had done so often during these past months since the first flight in.

This time there was no lazy circling of the compound and fearsome buzzing of the house. The little plane came over the compound, began its tight circle, and almost immediately they saw the inevitable bucket being lowered even before the circle pattern was properly set. The bucket gyrated wildly.

"Something's wrong," muttered Bill, almost to himself. But his wife heard him and a slight fear touched her heart. She waited while her husband walked slowly to what he called the target, his head uplifted, watching the bucket drop faster than he had ever seen it come before. It fell with a crash slightly outside the usual area, and Bill ran quickly to it as it hit the ground, rolled over, spilling out its plastic wrapped packet. It was still rolling when he fielded it expertly, and was tearing open the wrapping all in one motion, while the plane droned above him.

Quickly he scanned the hastily scribbled note: "Bill, you are needed at the Mennonite Mission where Max Wald has been killed and they don't expect Dorothea to live. Can you leave with me right away? Wave if you can.

Alan."

Without thinking, Bill's arm was in the air, and with the same motion he began to run towards his small hospital, calling for Baru as he did so.

With a sigh of relief the man in the plane saw the signal, began to reel in the rope and bucket, closed his window and pulled the plane out of its lazy circle.

As he turned to his controls, his eyes caught a brief glimpse of Jane still standing off to one side, and with a shock he remembered what this might mean to her. He hastily looked down again and saw Bill still racing towards the hospital, looked again at the woman standing alone and forlorn, then shrugged his shoulders.

"A life coming, a life going," he muttered to himself. "How do you choose? I'll wait and see what Bill does," and he set his plane for the rendezvous in the bush along the motor road.

# XIV

"Get my horse ready, Baru." The doctor's words were sharp and crisp, not with command, but with the sense of urgency that he felt. His African friend and evangelist knew too well that this was no "bwana" order of master to slave, and he turned and raced towards the stable huts, calling his sons to follow.

McAdams was under the pan roof verandah of the hospital in two strides, and into the cool surgery in a couple more. With the skill of long practice he picked up a small kit bag with its special compartments that he had had a local leather worker make for him, and with the other hand was reaching into drawers, boxes and cupboards for what he felt might be needed.

He became conscious of a slow plodding footstep, and turned to see his wife coming into the room, her bulk almost filling the doorway.

"You don't waste any time, do you?" she said as she came to his side, and with the familiarity borne of their years together, she began to take the instruments and bottles from his hands as he selected them, and placed them in the kit, in the exact places which he had long since shown her were the handiest for his use when he often had no one but Baru to help him. He couldn't afford the time of rummaging through the bag when death hovered close, as it often did. She had packed his bag in a score of other emergencies, and needed no directions for the task now.

Bill didn't reply. Through his mind were going all the items that he felt might fit any emergency, that so far to him was just a note in a bucket. He must be ready for anything, and he added some extra equipment, more scalpels, sutures and clamps than he would normally have taken. Then he looked around, and with a last gesture picked up a bottle of chloroform, and the small, compact mask in its sterile case, and handed them to his wife.

Only then did he speak to her, and as he did so, she saw the consternation that came into his eyes. With a jolt, he remembered. This could be the day for the birth of the baby, and the look in his eyes started the fear rising in hers.

Bill's hand went to his wife's shoulder and he stood for a moment before speaking. Then he was the calm, efficient surgeon again.

"I don't know what this will mean, Jane dear," and his fingers tightened on her shoulder so that she flinched. "This may be part of the Muslim uprising that Alan has been warning us about, but I must go. If Dorothea Wald is still alive I've got to do all I can to save her."

"Bill," she put up her hand and took his from her shoulder and held it tightly. "I know you must go. It's a life, and she is one of the Lord's servants. It's just that I'm afraid . . . there is a life here too," and she placed her hand over the unborn child. "What if he comes while you are away?" Fear began to rise in her voice making it shrill and catching.

"Jane dear. . . ." was man ever more torn between desire and duty? Who is most important, the unborn child or Dorothea? But even as the questions came to his mind, Bill knew what he must do.

"Jane dear," he went on, "I'm sure that you will be all right today. I'll send Alan back with a message as soon as I see what is wrong and how much time I will need, and I'll see that he gets messages to you and from you as frequently as possible. You'll be perfectly safe," and he took her into his arms, feeling the tremors that were beginning to come. "I'll give you a sedative so that you won't get restless and upset and hurry the pains. If anything does happen and I am not here, Baru and his wife have worked with me so often that I am sure you will be almost as safe with them as with me."

He paused. He remembered the talk at the breakfast table. What is this baby worth to me? And he remembered his reply "Everything."

Doctor and father. How do you choose? Yet even as the question rose again, he felt the trembling stop, looked down and saw Jane's mouth moving silently. She must have felt his gaze on her, for she looked up. Her eyes were tear dimmed, but serene.

"I know you must go, Bill. Dorothea needs you right now, and I will wait for you. I'll be all right. I promise. Go with God," and she added the phrase in Hausa, and lifted her face for her husband's kiss.

Holding her carefully in his arms Bill leaned down and kissed this woman who meant everything to him. He kissed her slowly, holding her gently as he did so, remembering the gift that God was waiting to give them.

Suddenly he lifted his head. "There's Baru with the horses," and he turned and picked up the full kit, and with his arm around his wife, turned and left the dispensary.

Baru was standing near the hospital entrance with two horses saddled, both nervously champing at the bit and pawing the earth.

"Guess they feel the atmosphere," was Bill's remark as he approached the horse that had taken him over hundreds of African miles. "They are extra frisky this morning. Well, we'll give them their heads, and let them run it off."

All the time he was speaking he was attaching his kit to the special straps at the back of the saddle. *How often he had used them during these past three years,* he thought. And each time, as now, the uncertainty of the emergency that was ahead, and the wife he was leaving behind kept gnawing at his mind, even while he drove his fingers to work with frenzied speed. As he worked at the saddle hitches, his horse kept swinging her head back, nudging his arm, as though she too felt the drama of the moment.

"Just another minute, old girl," he responded, slapping her belly with the flat of his hand. "Just another minute, and you can do your part," and with another slap, he finished the job and turned back to his wife.

"Baru will come right back," he said, taking her hand, "and if Alan has any more news, I'll also give him some instructions." He kissed her lightly on the lips, then swung up into the saddle. He saw the look on her face, knowing that she was holding back the tears that would have to flow as soon as he was out of sight. She was too far along, too highly strung, to take this easily, and his heart ached for her.

His horse began to dance sideways. He lifted his hand in a stiff salute, a salute that was just for her, shook out the reins over the horse's neck, gave a slight kick with his heels, and settled himself instinctively for the lunge that was the characteristic first pace that he had grown so used to. They whirled through the open gate of the compound, reached the straight stretch of the road with its mud hard packed by the burning sun, then settled to its long, free stride that would cover the ten miles in much less than the hour.

As he rode he recalled all he had heard of the growing discontent among the more fervid Muslims, and the increased tribal jealousies that had laid quiescent for nearly half a century. He also knew that there were many leaders who were becoming increasingly hostile and bitter at the number of people who were finding help at the Mission schools and clinics. And he knew that during this time of year tempers flared and danger lurked like a naked knife blade in the hands of a little child.

The single terse note was not entirely unexpected news, although he had not discussed with Jane the disturbing information passed on by Alan, particularly during these last months of her pregnancy.

At the thought of Jane his throat constricted. Instinctively he dug his heels into the flanks of his speeding horse. He would have to get Baru back to her as soon as possible. He trusted Baru as he had never trusted any other man. And with Baru and some of the other African men, Jane would be as safe as though he were at her side. "If only the baby is delayed a few days," and it seemed to be prayer from his heart.

The winds of change were sweeping this wonderful Africa with gale-like force. Where it would end, no one seemed to know. A rich country with a potential for development, and a people largely lovable, sometimes desperately needy, and occasionally, as now, caught in tides that seemed to be uncontrollable. And interwoven with it all were the tribal jealousies, the almost ferocious religious antagonisms, slanted largely at the Christian missionaries and their African co-laborers. Bill shuddered within himself. Knowing that he had only come with a great love in his heart, a love and a desire to help these wonderful people in this wonderful country, he ached with the desire to somehow let them know all this. He had nothing to gain for himself. He only wanted to help them find what he had found a few years before: peace and new life in Jesus Christ.

He pounded the saddle horn in frustration, only to clutch it in a life saving grip, as his horse shied as it had done before at the apparition of the plane, then stopped to dance in its fear and attempt to escape the strong hand that held the bit tight against the corners of his mouth.

# XV

Before Bill could dismount Alan was at his side holding the reins in an iron grasp. His face held no hint of humor now, only a bitterness and concern that surprised Bill. It transformed him.

He held the horse while Bill dismounted, then holding the reins loosely in his hands he turned to the doctor.

"Bill, I hate to ask you to leave this way, since I know that Jane must be near her time. Can you make it, or should you go back and be with her?" Concern was in his voice.

McAdams put a hand on his friend's shoulder. "Jane is too good a trooper to expect me to turn back when someone needs help. She knows I am a doctor and a missionary, and in these two jobs she knows that is something that takes precedence over her."

He began fumbling with the straps holding his kit to the saddle.

"And I'm no cold blooded medico either," he went on, as though he had anticipated a question. "Jane and I have a perfect understanding. She will be all right even if the baby does come before I get back. Baru who will be here in a minute or two, and his wife and one or two others have been trained in midwifery by me, and they know exactly what to do. But I think I'll get back," he added, pulling the sweat-stained bag from the horse's back. "Let's get this in the plane, and you tell me all you know, so I can send word back to her." And with that controlled speed that always seemed to move him when in an emergency, he turned to the plane leaving the pilot to tether the horse.

Even as he was doing it, Baru came around the last bend, this time approaching it slowly and cautiously. No more terrorized horses if he could help it. Bill McAdams smiled as he saw the look of caution and awe that still spread over the African's face as he came near to the plane. And this despite the past months of familiarity with it.

With the horses safely tethered, his medical kit in the small storage area behind the two seats. Bill turned to the pilot.

"Jane will want to know just what happened, and Baru can take back word if you can give it to me briefly."

"You remember Max Wald at the Mennonite Mission about 500 miles from here?" Bill nodded. He had heard about them, and also had heard about Max from Peter Dunning.

"He was a wonderful chap," went on Alan, "and he has been doing a terrific job despite opposition that came particularly from the Muslim community. Just a couple of days ago he received permission to open a school in the evenings and it seemed as though half the town wanted to register. Even some of the Muslims were sending their children to it. Today they were finishing the registering and one of the fanatical Muslims got into the line, killed Max and seriously wounded his wife Dorothea. I was contacted by radio to come and get you. They were unable to contact any other medical help, and evidently she is in desperate need. I think you will have to plan on surgery."

"I suppose," he went on, "that Jane could never make it to here and I could fly her to be with you?" and as he asked it he knew the question was foolish. Bill shook his head.

"This ten miles would be all that she would need to induce labor, and then it would be difficult. Thanks," and he put his hand on the pilot's arm. "I know that you are trying to help out in a difficult situation, but the only thing to do is fly me to Mrs. Wald as quickly as possible, and then we will either get back here, or figure out what is to be done."

Turning to Baru he spoke rapidly in Hausa, telling him what had taken place, and then adding his own instructions.

"Baru," and the doctor almost choked as emotion gripped him

momentarily, "we've been through a lot together. You have been closer than a brother to me and we have worked together and helped each other as brothers should. Baru," and his eyes misted slightly, "I've never needed you more than I do now. Jane is alone, and you know her **haifuwa** is close. Will you and your wife stay close to her, and if the baby begins to come, just do exactly as you have done when I have been with you before? You know where the midwifery box is, and everything you will need is in there. Baru," and he put his arm around the neck of the African, "all I love and have I put into your hands. Care for the **Uwar Gida** as you would care for me. I cannot repay you, but God will," and he gave the man's neck a squeeze.

Baru looked up at this man, whose skin was white but who had the voice and the heart of the blackman. Scores of times they had faced difficulty and danger. And in their service for Christ they had grown to know and love each other.

"My brother," and Baru used the term of closest relationship, "she will be as my own life, my own family. You can trust me, and," he added, "trust in the Lord, our **Ubangiji,** who will be with you and with us at the same time. Before you go in that **jirgin sama** that travels like a bird, let us pray here together, that God will give you skill and wisdom, and that He will care for the one you love."

Bill called Alan over, and the three men stood with their arms on each others' shoulders, they bowed their heads, and Baru prayed.

For Alan, only the occasional word was intelligible, but there was no need to translate the tone of voice, the reverence, the simplicity that poured from the heart of the African to the ear of God. For Bill, who had known this man from the day of his conversion, it was a shared prayer, a common burden that was left again where all problems and needs should go. It was a sacred trysting place in that small corner of the African jungle.

When he had finished with his fervent 'amin' in which the other men joined, Baru put out his hand to the two men, shook theirs solemnly, then turned back as they moved toward the plane.

"There's a man," commented Alan as they approached the plane together.

"Someday I'll tell you about Baru as I know him. I just wish I could write, for if there was ever a man whose story should be known to the world for its courage, dedication and sheer rich living, it's Baru, 'Having nothing yet possessing all things' as Paul put it. He's a wonderful man, a wonderful Christian and the closest thing to a brother that I will ever have."

They reached the plane, and Bill climbed in. Alan stooped to kick loose the blocks that he had forced under the wheels, slung them into the cabin by their connecting springs, then climbed in himself.

In a few minutes, the motor was warming up, the plane quivering to the tremendous build up of power, eager to be off and into its habitat of the clear blue sky. Alan eased off the brakes, gave it the throttle, and with his hands caressing the wheel, he maneuvered the plane down the bumpy road, gave it its head, and in a moment it was airborne, skimming the trees, banking into a tight circle as soon as it was safe to do so. He set the course westward. Down below, Baru shaded his eyes against the bright light of the sun, watched as the plane became a speck and then was lost to view. He turned to his horse, gathered up the reins of the other one, vaulted into the saddle with an agility that was ever the envy of his missionary friend, dug his bare heels into his horse's flank, and was soon racing back down the trail to the mission station and Jane.

# XVI

It was a remarkable scream. Wordless, primitive, sustained, it scarcely seemed human. Max Wald looked up from his desk for a moment, and felt a cold shudder go down his spine. Too often during these past days, had he heard the unearthly cry from the town, and each time a feeling of dread had come over him. During the past two years he had come to love this Africa with a passion he had not thought possible. But these last weeks—he shuddered.

He loved the people, the happy-go-lucky people, whose ready laughter and acceptance of their lot were a complete mystery to him. He found them so appealing and responsive, and he daily thanked God for the privilege of working among them.

"Perhaps they have never known any other kind of life," he had soliloquized, "but at the same time I don't know how they put up with all this hunger, squalor, ignorance and superstition. However, that's why I am here, and if I can be of any help to them at all, I'd gladly give my life to do it."

He bent his head over the desk again, and continued to write in the information of these students who were registering for the soon-to-be-opened school. It had been a long uphill fight, with almost the whole Muslim community against this Mission school, and the politicians and authorities wavering between what they knew was desperately needed and their own prejudice. Now reluctant permission had been given to open the school once again, and Max was eager to get on with the job.

One by one the students were being registered. They were all ages it seemed to him, many of them really too old for the elementary school work. Yet the hunger on their faces, the evident desire to learn to read 'the leaf that talks' kept him from questioning their ages too closely.

And these bright eyed little tykes, with their protruding tummies, many of them showing all too clearly the umbilical hernia that had resulted from careless midwifery. Some were clean, many were dirty. Some wore mere shifts of cloth, more holes than whole; others from affluent homes were neat and well dressed. . . . Max continued to write.

Shuffling up through the line came a furtive, older man, whose small stature hid him admirably among the younger people. Only his face, sleazy, lined and dull, made him stand out from the shuffling line of applicants. His long, loose robe was tucked up over his left shoulder, but the right side was completely covered, unlike the usual Muslim mode. As each student was registered, he shuffled closer and closer.

Once again the weird cry came up from the village, hovering in the morning air, bounced in echo from the nearby hill, then shuddered into silence. Again Max looked up, and beads of perspiration could be seen just below his hair line. For a moment he stopped his work and looked out at the line of those waiting to enter the school.

Dorothea, his wife, would soon be finished with the medical work she had outlined, and would be coming in to help him. Somehow he wished that she was here now. He wanted to hear her voice, see her in that white uniform that made her look like an angel of mercy. He smiled briefly, as he thought of saying that to her. Dear, practical Dorothea. She would only smile that big smile of hers that showed her even, white teeth against the deepening tan of her face, and go about her work.

Their ten years of married life had been rich and full. She had been good for him, and her solid, practical outlook had done much to stabilize him. *What a fortunate man he was,* thought Max. A wife, three children, and doing this job together. God had blessed them beyond measure. With a scarcely audible sigh, he turned to the next student, and began writing down the name, father's name, address, and previous schooling . . . if any, he always added.

Again he looked at the line of students, and roughly calculated how much longer it would take to register them. *No classes today,* he thought. It would take another hour to get all this information down and filed away. Then they would have to arrange the classes, set up the full school program to get this motley array of students started properly. Another hour, at least.

The shifty-eyed man moved closer. Now he was nearing the doorway, and an observer might have seen him reach inside his robe with his left hand, and adjust whatever he held with his right.

Thirty minutes . . . . . . . fifteen . . . . . ten . . . five . . . one . . . . . thirty seconds . . . . . fifteen . . . . . ten . . . . five . . . . . . three . . . . one . . . .

"Your name?" Max turned his head to see the next student in line, and an icy hand clutched momentarily at his heart as he saw the searing hatred, the bared teeth of the man towering over him. He tried to rise, found himself hampered, saw the flash of steel, felt the burning, stinging stab of pain in his back, gave a convulsive heave, and from his mouth came a cry . . . a wordless, sustained cry, then he slumped forward, scattering the papers that he had been filling in.

The silence that followed the cry was broken. This time it was by the man who had wielded the knife. With a bloodcurdling cry, and brandishing the dripping blade, he plunged for the door. The body of the missionary slumped from the table and slowly crumpled on to the floor, blood flowing from his back and mouth. He was dead.

As the assassin reached the door, his knife flashed, and those who had pressed in at the commotion and the screams jumped quickly to one side, and the man was through. Horrified eyes followed him as he sped across the compound.

Then another shout. Dorothea, doubtless attracted by the shrill screams, was standing in his pathway. Like an animal thirsting for blood, the man was upon her, his knife arm flashing up and down, once, twice, and she fell to the ground, now completely helpless. Again and again the knife flashed, each time leaving its line of blood on the arms and legs, as the woman vainly sought to dodge the attacker.

Suddenly some of the Africans moved, as though the shock of what they had seen had suddenly reached them. With stones and clubs they raced at the madman raining their missiles down on him until he cowered, then turned and fled into the town, a raging band at his heels.

Dorothea lay dazed. Her uniform had been slashed to ribbons, and the remnants were deeply dyed with blood. She tried to stand, dizzily pushing herself up from the ground. Then she looked down in horror. Hanging from her ripped abdomen she saw pulsing light pink intestines slowly oozing out. Cupping her hand over the gaping wound and the sickening sight, she began to stagger towards the hut.

"Max," these were the words that kept pounding through her mind driving off her own pain and shock. "Max, what has happened to Max?"

Her own eyes were glazed with pain and sweat. She felt only a tender arm around her shoulder, leaned against its owner with a sob of relief, and was slowly urged towards her house. "Max," her heart cried out, "Max, come, please come."

Then blessed oblivion.

# XVII

The two men in the plane were silent as Alan set his course for the west. He seemed to be physically urging his little plane on, and like a well trained horse, it was responding. At five thousand feet Bill saw the familiar landscape giving way to harsh bushland and great craggy outcroppings of rock.

"Barren place," remarked Alan at last, nodding his head downward, "I'd hate to set this plane down anywhere around here." He was busy for a few moments, then continued. "I wish that I had been able to get my stretcher fitted up for this flight. If we have to move Dorothea, it is going to be pretty hard on her. Perhaps we can fix up something back there," and he nodded to the storage area behind the cockpit.

Bill was silent, his mind on the emergency ahead, and constantly he thought of Jane, behind and alone on the station. His fingers beat a swift tatoo on his knee, and Alan seeing him thus engrossed in his thoughts, and guessing the reason for them, again fell silent. The little plane droned on.

Nearly two hours later Bill felt the plane dip slightly. He looked at the pilot and saw him staring ahead and down. Following his eyes Bill picked out the faint glimmer of sun reflecting from a pan roof.

"That it?" he asked at last.

"Just beyond those buildings there is a playing field where the kids have been playing soccer. In their bare feet at that," he added. "I can put her down there and perhaps they will have some way of getting you back to the house. It's about a mile back." Again he fell silent, busy at the thing he knew best, and Bill could feel the plane respond to his light touch.

His first pass over the field quickly cleared it of the curious Africans who had raced out at the sound of the plane, and they saw one man waving some wandering goats off of the improvised landing strip.

On his second run, Alan skimmed the trees that bordered the field, barely missed a towering goal post made of great bamboo shoots tied in bundles, and then the plane was down with its familiar three skips, a series of short bumps, then rolling smoothly to a stop.

"Almost made a goal on that one," the irrepressible Alan was unbuckling his lap straps, while he pointed to the goal posts only a few yards away. "Give me another couple of feet and I could fly this thing right through," and he chuckled as he opened the door.

McAdams only gave a slight smile to the comments, then he was following the pilot out of the plane. On the ground they were met by another missionary who introduced himself as Max Wald's associate, then led them to a Jeep that was parked at the edge of the field.

"We're afraid that Dorothea has been fatally wounded," he began as they settled into the Jeep. "We buried Max about two hours ago, after the local authorities got here and took down all the particulars."

He stopped talking to weave his way skillfully around a herd of goats that bleated and ran into the bush. "Did Alan tell you what happened?"

"Just that Max Wald was killed and his wife seriously hurt," he replied.

"It's a bad business," the man shook his head. "It seemed as though we were off to a great start, and although there have been rumblings for the past several months we thought it was just talk. Now we know that it is more . . . although I will say that so far this has stirred up more concern and interest for our work than we ever had before."

"You know," he went on, as he passed through a gate, and drove along a driveway lined with sickening-sweet, pink oleander, "we have wept until there are no tears left, for we feel keenly the loss of Max, and perhaps Dorothea. But someone was saying that many things can work out for the furtherance of the Gospel when we often only think they are hindrance and loss. If this is so, then Max will not have died in vain. . . . Here we are," and he braked the Jeep to a stop in a flurry of gravel.

The men bounded out of the car and followed him quickly into the whitewashed building. "We brought Dorothea in here. Let us know if there is anything else you want."

"Let me wash up first and then I'll see her." Bill was stripping off his bush jacket while he spoke, dropping it on a chair as he was led into a small washroom.

While he scrubbed his fingers and arms he issued orders for hot water, and something to use as a sterilizer.

"We have a pressure cooker, will that do?" asked the man anxiously.

"The very thing," replied Bill. "Put about a cupful of water in it and get it boiling fast. Let me know when it is ready."

Carefully drying his hands, he turned, and without a word the man led him into the room where a woman was lying on the bed, its covers stained with blood, her fingers twitching on the sheet that covered her.

Bill have never seen Dorothea Wald before, and as he went to the bedside he looked at her closely.

He saw a small boned, dark woman, who was pretty but not beautiful. The skin on her face was waxen white, and her dark hair piled in confusion around her head on the pillow. Her eyes were wide with questioning as he approached the bed. She was not unconscious. Good.

With a hint of a smile on his face, he leaned over the bed, and the fearful look in the woman's eyes suddenly disappeared. A weak smile answered his, then he was too busy to look into her face any longer.

Lifting the sheet, he exposed the cruelly torn flesh of her

abdomen, the great gaping wound extending across it for several inches. Hanging on the wound throbbing with pulse beats were the pink intestines. One of her arms tried to move across in modesty. He gently took the arm in his hand, noting as he did so that great gashes stretched on it from elbow to wrist. For a moment fury blazed in him at the man who could thus treat a woman. Then he was all doctor. All business.

Barking out crisp commands he set to work. He scarcely noticed that Alan was standing nearby, and that another woman had also come into the room. Both of them responded to his orders, as with grim determination he began to work over the woman who seemed so close to death.

He treated her for shock, gently pressing the needle's point into one of the small ungrazed areas of her upper arm, ordered heat around her, and waited for his drug to take effect before turning his attention to the great, gaping abdominal wound. He groaned inwardly at the lack of equipment on hand, quickly substituting and extemporizing as he worked with skill and speed.

It was more than two hours later that he finally straightened up. The neatly stitched and clamped incision hid the ugliness of what the flashing knife had done. He was sure that there was no infection, and he had been able to stop the internal bleeding, and suture the lacerated flesh. Now time alone would tell if he had been successful.

He turned his attention to the gashes on the arms. While he was doing it, the other woman lifted the sheet from off her legs, and he saw that the knife had also inflicted large though not serious wounds there as well. Quickly he cleansed, then sewed them up, then bandaged them skillfully from the rapidly dwindling rolls in his kit.

When he had finished, he brushed his hand wearily over his eyes, and turned, almost bumping into Alan as he did so.

"Good flying, Bill," the accolade did not seem out of place. "Come on out for some coffee."

Bill nodded numbly. For a moment he paused, gave an order

to the missionary who had assisted him, then turned and almost stumbled from the room. The stomach wrenching strain that he could never get used to made him feel weak and dazed. Alan took his arm and led him out of the room.

The coffee was hot and strong and Bill drank it down gratefully. As he felt warmth flooding through him and the stimulant taking effect, the cloud seemed to lift from his mind. He turned to the missionary who had met them at the playing field.

"She will have to stay very quiet for a couple of days," he said, "then if she can be moved we should get her to a hospital or someplace where she can get some continuing attention." He stopped as the man shook his head.

"There's no place where we could get her that kind of attention," he said, throwing his hands wide. "We will do our best for her here if you tell us what we are to do."

Bill shook his head. "She will need professional help, particularly if infection shows. There is nothing nearby?" and the man shook his head.

"Bill," Alan had laid a hand on his shoulder. "Would we have a week?"

"No more," replied the doctor. "If you can get me in here two or three times in that week, I will be able to look after her. But it would be impossible to keep that up for more than a week or so."

"All I need," replied Alan.

Bill looked at him questioningly. "My airborne ambulance," Alan replied to the unspoken question. "Give me a couple of days, and I'll have the plan rigged up and we can take her wherever you want."

"Such as . . . ?" dryly Bill's question came out. Alan looked crestfallen. Then he brightened. "Such as your place," he said jubilantly. "I told you you needed an air strip, and it has to be done. Get Baru to round up a gang, and you can give me a fairly smooth landing strip right near the house. Then she will be right where you can keep an eye on her," and he looked his delight.

Bill pondered it for a minute, then he nodded. "A week will tell us which way things will go with her," and he nodded back to the room he had just left. "I don't know how much damage the shock has done to her, seeing her husband killed and being nearly killed herself. She seems to be a plucky girl, and if she can hold on for the next few days I have high hopes."

His eyes lightened. "Tell you what," he said. "You head back to the Mission, and tell Jane what has happened. Ask her to get Baru, and have him do exactly what you tell him to do. I'll stay close here today and tomorrow, then you can fly me back there. If everything is o.k. here," he added.

Volkes nodded his head. "They have a good supply of gasoline here," he said, "so I should be able to run a taxi service. . . ." he caught himself in time as he saw the other missionary looking at him askance. Bill grinned, and felt the stiffness begin to leave his face. What a treat it was to have this fellow around. He quickly wrote a note to Jane, handed it to the pilot, and watched him leave, his loose kneed shuffle more pronounced than ever. Bill knew that despite his carefree manner he too felt the tragedy and suspense of this jungle drama.

He turned back into the sick room.

# XVIII

During the next few days Bill was able to see what kind of a man Volkes really was. Working some fifteen hours a day, his hands moving with the precision and skill of a surgeon, he was able to outfit his 'airborne ambulance' within the week. During that time, Dorothea was making such excellent progress that Bill had been able to make a trip back to his own mission to see how Jane was making out.

He had found her becoming increasingly nervous and was grateful for the fact that he would soon be back. Having the two patients under one roof would make it a lot easier to care for them. He checked Jane thoroughly before leaving to bring Mrs. Wald to the station, and assured her that everything was fine.

"Just don't have twins while I'm away," his concern was hidden under the banter. "Alan and I will be back in about 36 hours, depending on Dorothea's condition. Then I can look after both of you here," and he kissed her forehead, finding it hot and sweating as he did so. "No pains yet?" he asked.

Jane shook her head. "I just want you nearby Bill," and she held his hand tightly. "Sometimes I get a little bit afraid," and her eyes were round and bright.

"Nothing to this baby business," he replied. "People have been having them since almost the beginning of time." She didn't smile, and he dropped his banter. "Seriously Jane, you are in excellent shape. The baby's heartbeat is steady, and there is every evidence of a good, safe delivery. Now let's just pray together before I go. The Lord is more concerned in this than I am, and we can safely leave everything to Him." So saying, he knelt beside her chair, and simply and movingly prayed. As he did so, Jane felt the trembling that had begun, start to subside, and before he was through she felt a rush of peace and contentment that she had not known since she had been left alone several days before.

"It's wonderful to know the Lord and to have Him enter into our lives," she said when her husband was finished praying. "I wonder what people do that don't have Him to turn to."

"I could tell you that," replied her husband. "When I was in practice at home, I found that people who had no spiritual foundation at all, wore themselves out physically and emotionally, and it seemed that only drugs could substitute for the abnormal strain. I often prayed with patients and talked to them of the spiritual resources available, and when they were responsive half of their problem was taken away. Now I have to go," he took her into his arms, and kissed her. "Alan is waiting for me. The next time we fly in it will be on our own airstrip that Baru has nearly completed. I think we will keep Dorothea Wald here in the house," and his wife nodded her agreement, "rather than up at the hospital. I think she will need company as much as medical help. Her children will have to stay back at the mission, but the folks there will look after them until she is strong enough to go home. See you in the next day or so. Take care," and with a wave of the hand he was gone. Soon she heard the horses' gallop, and then turned back into the house. Loneliness swept over her like a tidal wave, and she busied herself with getting a room ready for Dorothea, moving with the heavy rolling tread of the mother-to-be. Keeping her hands busy kept the feeling of aloneness at bay.

The plane was waiting for Bill as he rode up the road. The horses were now fairly familiar with the strange thing in the trail, and it took him just a few moments to unstrap his kit, turn his horse over to the African who had accompanied him, then he was in the plane with Alan. The takeoff was without incident, and soon they had their course set for the Mennonite Mission.

"Everything all right with Jane?" asked Alan when he could turn from his instruments.

"Just fine," replied the other. "She is becoming increasingly nervous as the time approaches, and I can't say that I blame her. Another couple of days and it should be over, if our reckoning is correct. I sure hope that all that stuff we ordered from home gets here on time. Perhaps if Jane had it now it would keep her occupied and interested. As it is she can't do much work, and when she just sits and thinks, without me around . . . well, it's pretty hard."

"Sure is," agreed the other. "She keeps up a good front when we are away, but those rings under her eyes didn't come from sleep at night."

Bill nodded. The mission was now in sight and he watched with fascination as the pilot brought the little plane down.

Behind the cockpit was the little ambulance compartment that Alan had contrived, with the stretcher bolted firmly down, and the great web straps that would soon hold the patient, now neatly folded on its blanket. Bill had made every test he could think of to ensure that his patient would be safe and had congratulated Alan on the excellent job he had done.

The latter disclaimed credit. "Just one of the things I learned in the air force," he said. "Several times we had to improvise to take care of the wounded. I'm glad that the experience can be used for something like this. How is the airstrip coming along?" he asked.

"It will be ready when we return," replied McAdams. "Baru has done a magnificent job as usual, and he has the place as smooth as a table top. A few rains will finish that," he added with a grin, "but for this first landing things should go smoothly. If you can remember how to get it down safely, that is," as the plane bucked, then swooped up under full power.

Alan waved his hand. "Well I'm learning," he chuckled. "Now if those silly goats would only learn," and he pointed to some that were feeding blissfully on the playing field. They watched while the goatherd chased them off, waving his long, spear-like stick at them, then Alan circled for the second run. "If I make any mistakes let me know," he added.

"Shall I tell you before or afterwards?" countered his friend.

"That's the trouble with mistakes. You can't do anything about them before they happen, and if it's in a plane, you can rarely do anything about correcting them afterwards."

"So don't make any this time, please. Remember I'm a father-to-be." Both men laughed. The plane settled down easily as it touched the field. "Minus my three special bumps this time," said Alan with ill-concealed pride. "Just to show you I can do it when you have your passenger on board."

The two men clambered out of the plane, and soon were in the Jeep and heading to the Mission. The big test was yet to come.

Bill walked into the room where his patient was lying. She had come out of shock, the wounds were healing without infection, but only X-rays would tell if there was any internal damage. As soon as she could travel Bill knew that she would have to be flown home. Now his concern was for her own attitude, as she became fully aware of the extent of the tragedy that had overtaken her.

He had nerved himself somewhat, as he prepared to enter the room. "Perhaps I can be of some help to her spiritually," he thought to himself. Voicing a silent prayer, he entered.

A smiling face was turned to him, and Dorothea's face was alight. "Hi, Dr. McAdams," was her greeting, her voice somewhat low pitched.

"It's Bill," he countered, "and hi to you. How are you doing?"

"Just fine thanks. I've had such a wonderful sleep. But more wonderful, I have been lying here thinking how privileged we are." As the quizzical look that crossed his face, she added, "Yes, I know Max is dead. I think I knew it all the time, but I asked about it this morning and they told me." Still no shadow crossed her face, the smile remaining bright, but not with the fixation of being forced. Her eyes were shining and her whole appearance was one of joy.

"Bill, I think you wonder if I need sympathy. Well, it's nice to have understanding friends, but when Max and I came out here it was with the full knowledge and realization that 'Christ must be magnified whether by life or by death.' We have faced the possibility of trouble and death for the past six months. And I can honestly say that I just feel humbled and grateful that the Lord should honor us in this way. I'm sure I speak for Max too . . . he wouldn't have wanted anything but the will of God. Do you know, Bill," and just for a second her breath caught, then she went on, "the Thursday before he was killed, Max was speaking to a small group of us about the persecution of the early church. And he said that we had not yet suffered real persecution. Then the day before he died, he preached about what he called the 'high cost of low Christian living.' I'm sure that he felt that the Lord was going to do something to show what real Christian living is, 'whether by life or by death.' I don't think that Max really knew what price he would have to pay, but I do know he was ready to pay any price. And so was I," she added simply.

Bill felt the burning of tears behind his eyelids. She went on, "It is true that little did I think that God would ask this of us, yet, in one way I feel honored that God could count us worthy of sacrifice. I know that God has His purpose in all of this and I am willing to face the future, lonely, as I know it will be at times, with a courage and trust in God who has been so close to me." Her face began to crumple slightly, then the look was gone, and she smiled again. "You don't mind me talking this way to you, do you?"

Bill could only shake his head. He had seen people with souls naked before, but never had he seen such courage and faith. He was almost overwhelmed.

She went on, "I have been trying to look into the future, and am really surprised that I have no sense of despair or fear at all. I know that the road ahead will not be easy, but I know that God is sufficient for everything. You know what Bruce, my oldest son said?" and her face lighted again at the memory. "To-day when he was in to see me, he said: 'Mother, when I get big, I am coming back here to tell the people about Jesus, the way Daddy was doing it.' You know, the Bible is right when it talks about the faith of a little child. It is only since I have felt very childlike during these days that real peace and contentment have come."

She stopped talking, and Bill silently reached over and took the hand that was lying outside the coverlet. Surreptitiously he took her pulse, and felt a strong, steady beat. He smiled back at her.

"Dorothea," he began, "I thought that today would be a hard day with me trying to console and encourage you. Instead of that, you have encouraged me. And I'm grateful. Our own problems seem small when compared with what has happened to you."

All the time he was talking, he was removing the great wide belt of a bandage that covered the incision, and noted the healthy pink flesh that was forming. "Your heart is o.k., your courage is high, and your wound is healing. The Lord is good," and she smiled back at him.

"Now," he went on, "our plans are to move you so that I can watch you for the next couple of weeks. Will you mind being separated from the children for awhile? The folks here said that they would look after them, while we keep you under surveillance for awhile anyway. We can fly you to our station and then when you can travel, Alan Volkes will fly you into the railhead where you can get a plane home." He paused for a moment, then went on: "My wife is expecting a baby sometime soon, so I'll have the two of you to look after and you can console each other," and he busied himself putting a fresh dressing over the wound. "I'll strap you up a little tighter for the trip out," he explained as she complained of the pressure, "so just bear with it for awhile."

He put a thermometer into her mouth, openly took her pulse,

and entered the record on the chart. "Not bad, not bad," he murmured so that she could hear. "Pulse normal, temp. still up, everything under control." He set the record down. "We'll leave before noon tomorrow," he went on "so whatever you want to take with you, have your friends here get it ready. Try to travel light though," he admonished, "you won't need many clothes this trip." They laughed. "You can also have the rest of your things packed from here and sent upcountry to wait for you there. Or better still, they can be sent with your children when they go in. Now I'll leave you for awhile. Don't get all excited, and undo all that has been done. I'll come in later." He turned to go.

"Doctor," he turned back. She was lying with a hand stretched out to him. He took it in his own. "Is there a possibility that I can come back here and continue the work Max was doing?"

"I can't answer that," he replied. "Several things will have to be thought through. Your children," she nodded, "your health . . . oh a lot of things. But remember what you said about the will of God?" Again she nodded. "Then your future is involved in that too. He doesn't make mistakes."

"Thanks . . . and Bill, thanks for your help and care. I know something of what it means for you to be away just now. I'll be ready tomorrow." This time he left the room.

# XIX

It was getting late the next afternoon when Alan appeared at the Mission house and motioned to Bill to meet him outside. Dorothea was in a light sleep and the doctor moved quietly to the door and slipped out.

"Can we get away soon?" was the quiet query of the pilot. "The plane is all ready and I'm just a little bit afraid that we might not be able to land if the light isn't good. You are in a pretty dense part of the bush and the airstrip might have too much shadow for a safe, smooth landing."

"I think we can leave in about half an hour," replied Bill. "I have just given Dorothea a sedative, and as soon as it takes hold, we will put her on the stretcher and get her to the plane. I'm afraid the Jeep would be too much for her, so I'll get some of the men to carry her. It's only a mile or so, and it will be a lot smoother, even if it takes us a while longer."

"Fine," replied the other. "That means we can lift off in about an hour and a half," and he squinted at the sun. "Make it a little sooner if you can."

McAdams turned back into the room, and whispered some orders to the two missionaries, relaying his request for carriers for the stretcher and the bags that Mrs. Wald would take.

"I have the men right here who will do it," replied the man, "so anytime you are ready, we are."

"Good," the doctor stepped to the bed, lifted the eyelid of the patient, then nodded with satisfaction. "Let's get going then."

After placing the patient on the stretcher, they moved out of the room. As soon as they reached the outside, Bill shaded her face with a wide brimmed helmet so that the sun would not startle her awake. The four carriers were soon moving smoothly and evenly down the road towards the playing field. Bill walked beside the patient, one hand holding her wrist, the other holding the shading hat.

They were soon at the plane, and Alan, who had been standing anxiously near the cockpit door left it to meet them near the edge of the field.

"I'll direct them in getting the stretcher inside," he said to the doctor, "so be sure when you tell them what to do, that you get it to them straight. It would be grim to have them do it wrong."

"No fear," replied the other. "You just say the word or motion with your hand, and they'll do it."

On reaching the plane, the men set their load down. Bill was trying to catch his breath as they did so, and he noticed that they were not even breathing heavily. On orders from Alan, the men stooped again, this time raising the stretcher high above their heads in one synchronized motion as though they had been trained in putting stretchers into planes.

Bill noticed that the cockpit door was off and one of the seats removed. On orders relayed from Alan, the men, still keeping the patient high, moved towards this gap, while Alan scrambled in ahead of it, grasped the carrying handles, and together the men eased the stretcher into the plane. It was such a smooth operation that Alan grinned as he came out.

"All battened down," he saluted first the doctor then the carriers. "Now to put the door back on, and bolt the seat down, and we will be ready to roll."

Bill turned to the missionaries who were watching. "We'll keep you informed about Dorothea as often as we can," he said kindly. "Look after the children, and when she can move we will make some plans about getting them all home."

They shook hands, and with a "God bless you all," Bill turned to the plane, where Alan was waiting for him to get in. When the two were settled down, Bill looked back and saw that Dorothea was sleeping quietly, and he signaled for the lift off. The plane responded to the careful piloting of Volkes, and soon they were airborne, and heading back to the east.

Bill turned in his seat to keep an eye on his patient. The two men were silent as they sped back. A slight haze gave the ground below an ethereal look and occasionally the pilot noticed his landmarks were blotted out. But Alan had flown the course too often to lose his way, and alternately watching his compass and seeking his markings, he soon saw the 'takama' hill, with its jaunty tilt looming up out of the mist. He gave it a wide berth, picked out the break in the jungle that denoted the mission station, and swung around to take advantage of the wind drift as he checked for the newly laid out airstrip. He felt Bill's hand jogging his arm and followed his pointing finger. There, about the size of the playing field that they had left, he saw the newly cleared area, now smooth, the freshly hoed earth standing out in bright contrast to the dark, undisturbed earth and the shadow of the jungle that surrounded it.

Alan examined the ground carefully as he dropped lower, skimming just above the tree level. There must be no mistake, he thought to himself. The ground looked good, and he swung around again, to come down wind. The descent at the beginning of the field would have to be steep, since they had been unable to get more trees out of the way for the run. But he felt that he could do it. The plane needed only a short space to drop down.

Down, down he came, then at about two hundred feet he slowly eased back just as the tail assembly flicked at the top of a giant dum dum palm. Bill felt his hands sweating, then he grinned at the skill of the pilot.

*Each to his own,* he thought, as he felt the plane settle down slowly and with scarcely a bump, then begin rolling towards the far side, gently slowed by the pressure of the brakes. "I'd rather sew up a severed muscle or nerve end anytime," and his hand hit Alan playfully on the shoulder by way of commendation.

With the plane stopped, Alan turned to his companion. "Where shall we unload?" he asked.

Bill looked around. "Taxi back about half way," he pointed to the place where a wide path appeared in the trees, now jammed with Africans as they raced to see this bird from the sky so close up. "Baru will be there and he will have some men ready."

Swinging the plane around as though on an axis, the pilot brought it close to the milling group who drew back hesitantly as it approached them.

"Where's Baru?" asked Bill, somewhat querulously. Alan shrugged his shoulders by way of reply.

With the plane stationary he opened the door and stepped down, followed by Bill. He saw one of the dispensers standing nearby and called him over.

"Where's Baru?" he asked. The man looked at him for a moment, then replied:

"The **Uwar gida** began her pains a little while ago, and Baru felt he should stay, and that I should tell you that so far she is all right."

Volkes saw the look on Bill's face. "Is Jane all right?" he asked anxiously.

"It looks as though labor pains have started," said Bill, spinning on his heel and racing toward the plane. "I'll get you some men. Can you see about getting Dorothea back to the house?" He didn't wait for a reply. He was at the plane, and in a moment reappeared with his medical kit.

Slipping a strap over his shoulder, he spoke rapidly to the dispenser telling him to do whatever the pilot signaled him to do, and to get Dorothea to the mission with as little trouble as possible.

Suddenly he caught himself, stifling the momentary anxiety that he had felt at the news of Jane. Then he went back to the plane, slipping the pack off his shoulder as he did so. He had a patient here for whom he was responsible. Quickly he climbed back into the small cockpit, and found Dorothea wide awake and curious.

"You all right, Dorothea?" he asked anxiously. He would have preferred to have her sleep through this period.

"Just fine thanks, Bill. I woke up when we were starting down-hill," and she smiled. "I didn't even feel a bump when we landed."

"Alan landed like a thistledown," he smiled back at her. "Any pain?"

"I know that I have felt better," she replied.

"Will you need a sedative. I can give you one now, and it will be easier for you if they jostle you at all."

"Thanks, Bill," she replied. Then she saw Alan's head peering over his shoulder. "But if Alan can put a big plane down that easily, he can take care of my one hundred and eight pounds," and she smiled at the other man.

The pilot looked at her white face and beaming eyes, and felt a slight constriction in his throat. "I'll see you are cared for, ma'am," he said. Then he added, "Bill has just had word that Jane is in labor, but he wouldn't head home until he was sure you were all right. Are you?"

She was instantly all concern. "Get out of here, but fast," and the concern was evident in her face and eyes. "We'll get along just fine."

With relief Bill slipped out of the plane, jostled through the knot of men who had appeared at the command of the dispenser, picked up his kit, and began to dogtrot rapidly away from the plane. All he could see now was Jane, waiting and wondering, as the pains of motherhood claimed her. His feet began to move faster, and soon he was loping with giant strides towards her.

"Coming Jane," his heart seemed to beat out the words, and his feet picked up the tempo "Jane . . . Jane . . . Jane . . . Jane. . . ."

# XX

Jane listened until the hoof beats had died away, then she moved listlessly back into the house, while one of the school girls came in and began to clear up the dishes. The girls had volunteered to help the **Uwar gida** until her baby should arrive. Jane had been most grateful and touched.

She wandered into the bedroom and began making the bed, hindered by her bulk from bending over too much, and feeling and looking awkward at doing this, the most housewifely of chores. She smiled as she remembered some of the bantering from Bill at her attempts to do some of the tasks that she had done so easily for years.

Suddenly she stopped, stricken. A knife-like pain had come and gone like a flash of light, leaving her gasping, perspiration starting out on her forehead.

"Have they started?" and for a moment fear clutched her. Alone . . . what would she do? Fighting down the panic that threatened to engulf her, she sat down for a moment waiting to see if the pain occurred again. One minute, two minutes, three minutes, and still she sat. There was no repeat, and finally she relaxed, her hands stopped trembling, and she wiped the sweat from her face with a gesture that was one of relief.

She finished making the bed, then went out to the kitchen. Standing in the doorway was Baru, his arms folded, the look of concern on his face that always settled on him when this wife of his friend was alone on the station.

She looked at him for a moment, then breathed a prayer of

thanksgiving that there was such a man nearby. Baru was the one whom she had heard about long before she came to Africa. Her husband always spoke of him with such feeling and affection that he seemed to be part of their family rather than one of another race and color.

Color? For a moment Jane thought of the word. She looked at this man with his black skin. Color? It was only a skin pigmentation as she had often heard her husband say. They were of one blood, and this man was a brother beloved.

"Christians are color blind," Bill had said on one occasion when he had been distressed by the news from other places, of segregation, hatred and racial strife. "There are good and bad whites and good and bad blacks. As well as yellow and brown," he had added. "I don't see why a man can't be accepted on his own merits instead of on the color of his skin or on the extent of his culture. When the family of God is chosen, as the Bible says, 'out of every nation, kindred, people and tongue,' we have to accept them as brothers. Or else," he added with a grin, "heaven is going to be a difficult place to enjoy. I'm sure that the Lord isn't going to divide heaven into color sections. People are fighting so much about differences down here," he went on, "that I am sure that if it all followed them to heaven, their mansions would have to be split-level," and she had had to laugh at the joke.

Jane was amazed at her own acceptance of African life and people. To be sure it was a strange and different culture. There were stone age primitives that she had seen while on trek with her medical missionary husband. And she had seen the superstition that kept the mortality rate so high, particularly with babies and children.

She would never forget the time that a woman had come to the compound hospital when she was helping with the sudden influx of those sick. She had been in the long line of patients that Jane was checking and assigning to the proper area for treatment.

She had taken the woman's name and area where she lived,

and had asked what help she needed, when the woman replied offhandedly:

"Oh it's not me. It's my baby here," and she had opened her sarong and disclosed the small yellow soled feet of a baby that was slung on her back.

At Jane's request, the woman undid the cloth strap that held the baby in place, and swung the mite around for the missionary to see.

The child was wizened and undersized. Its age was hard to guess, perhaps three, perhaps six years of age. Swathed around the baby's head was a filthy cloth from which only one eye peeped out, an eye that was lackluster and dry. *Even tears were beyond the little thing*, thought Jane, and it certainly was not terrified at being thus held on display as most of the African children would have been.

Calling to one of the nursing assistants that Bill had trained, Jane asked her to take off the cloth from around the child's head so that they could examine it.

With the mother holding the infant in her arm, the nurse had slowly unwrapped the cloth to disclose the face, one half, including one eye, completely hidden by a large banana leaf. As Jane looked, she suddenly felt a surge of sickness within her. From under the banana leaf, released from the pressure of the cloth, there came wriggling a small white maggot to be followed by another. Then as the leaf was stripped off Jane turned away gagging.

Covering the banana leaf was a mixture of some black substance and cow manure, and in this the maggots were alive, now wriggling to get away from the light that glared down on them. But the face itself: from the temple to the chin, and from the ear to the corner of the mouth, it was a great, gaping, superating ulcerous mass so obscene that even the hardened African nurse cried out in horror.

The one eye seemed loose in the red and white socket, with the eyeball itself inflamed to such a degree that pupil and white blended into one mass of fiery color.

When she had control of herself Jane began to record the case. Then she asked: "What happened?"

Almost nonchalantly the woman told of taking her daughter to the local witch doctor to have the tribal marks carved into her face. Jane could almost see it, as she had once before. The child had been lying on the ground, and the bony knees of the witch doctor pressing into the little forearms to prevent movement. Then the flash of a knife blade, the press into unresisting young flesh, the spurt of blood and the scream of the startled child. Then incision after incision until the face streamed with blood, and the geometric pattern of the centuries-old tribal marks appeared, crude and rough against the red stain.

Reaching a gnarled hand over, the witch doctor had scraped some oily soot from the bottom of a cooking pot, and still holding the girl, had rubbed it carefully into the wounds, packing them until the blood was stenched.

When the little girl was finally allowed to rise she stood there with the great welts running across her cheeks and forehead, marked forever, branded like an animal.

Soon the sores would welt over, and if all was well, the great black marks would heal, distinguishing the features for all to see.

The story that the woman now told her followed the same pattern. With one difference.

"One side healed up," she had said touching the right side of the cheek. "This other would not heal," and she had no word for infection. "I took her back to the **mai tsafi** the witch doctor, and he made some other medicine from this cow manure and urine. When I saw that the sore was nibbling at the corner of her eye I was afraid that her eye would drop out. So I have come to the place where they tell me you make people better," and she tried to hand Jane her baby.

Jane was tempted to take it, then realized that the mother would have to be with it, take care of it, and follow the doctor's instructions. She spoke to the nurse who took the mother and baby directly into the hospital where Bill was seeing the more urgent cases.

"Jesus said, 'Suffer the little children to come unto Me'," murmured Jane to herself, "but how often out here that is turned around to say, 'the little children suffer'! You are the only One that can help them," and she turned back to her work.

It was some months later, when visiting with Bill in the out-patients' sick huts, that she saw the woman again. Her face was beaming as she pointed to her daughter squatting nearby, helping to grind their evening corn. At the greeting, the little girl looked up. The great ulcer on her face was now healed and a wrinkled layer of pinkish skin covered that once ghastly hole. The eyes were bright and beaming, the little body filled out with healthy flesh.

"Later we will cover the patch with a skin graft," said Bill as he had knelt down beside the girl. "But something better has happened. Ask the mother how she is," and he turned back to the child.

Jane did as she was asked. The woman clasped her hands a moment, then quietly replied. "When I first came here, if you had asked me how I was, I would have answered in the words and custom of my people, 'I am well.' But I wasn't well, I was in darkness. Now I have heard the **Bature Mai Magani** speak," and she looked over at the 'white doctor' still checking her daughter. "I have heard his words and I have seen him work. He has given me light," and she placed her hand over her heart. "Light inside, and that light is Yesu Kristi," and she let her head drop. Then she looked up at Jane. "When I first talked to you I was a pagan, and followed the **tsafi** of my people. Now I am a Christian and will follow the way of Jesus," and her face beamed.

*No*, thought Jane to herself, as she now stood looking at Baru for a moment, with these pictures flashing through her mind, *it isn't color. It's Christ. He makes all the difference, and makes us all one in Him.*

She spoke to Baru for a few moments, then he said to her: "**Uwar gida**, my friend the **Likita** has asked me to care for you while he is gone. This I will do. Each day I will be just outside the door here, and at night I will sleep nearby. My brother trusts me to care for you, and for him and for Christ whom we both love I will do it. When you need me, I will be here, as will Kimbiya, my wife." She looked past him and saw his wife sitting under a mango tree, their sleeping mats spread out and a few household items nearby.

"But you can't sleep there," she said. "If you and Kimbiya are going to be here, I want you near," and she smiled. "There is a room here for you both, and while I know you cannot sleep on our type of beds, you bring your own in and fix it up as you will." She felt a great relief. It was being alone in the house that she feared most. Now she would have company.

Baru started to argue, hesitated and stopped. He knew that Jane would feel better with someone nearby, and with a nod he turned and called to his wife. Together they brought in their mats and the other items into the guest room, pushed the white man's bed to one side, and placed their own mats on the cement floor. Suddenly Baru put his hand under the mat and shook his head.

"Too cold," Jane heard him mutter as he left the room. He was back soon, this time carrying his ingeniously constructed cornstalk bed, put it down, and brought in another for his wife. With their mats spread over them, he patted them lovingly. "Better than the white man's soft bed," he said grinning at Jane. "My back would bend and never straighten if I tried to sleep on that," and he gestured to the bed they had pushed to one side.

"And I would never sleep if I slept on that bed of yours," said Jane in return. The three of them laughed, and Jane left to plan her meals for the day.

"No color," she kept saying to herself. "No color, just brothers and sisters under the skin . . . and in the heart," she added.

# XXI

It was the same knife-like pain that stabbed Jane awake. With a suppressed cry lest she waken Bill, she rolled over in a moment of agony, only to feel the emptiness of the bed beside her. Realization that she was alone swept over her and her hand groped for the small light beside the bed, its power fed by the generator that had made such a difference in their bush home for the past three years.

The light came on, its orange tinged glow gradually brightening as the bulb heated. She sat up in bed, once more suffused with sweat from pain and the fear that gripped her again as it had done that morning. She looked towards the window and saw the purple shades of the dawning morning. Night was gone. Would Bill be back before it came again? A prayer welled out from suddenly chattering lips and she laboriously slipped out of bed.

The slight creaking of the bed must have done it, for the next moment a voice came through the partially closed door.

"Is everything well, **Uwar gida**?" It was Baru's voice, low pitched with concern. Despite her fear, Jane had to smile at her 'watch dog.'

"I just had a sudden pain," she replied, "but it is nothing." She added hurriedly, "it has not come again. I will go back to bed again," and she heard him turn back and speak to Kimbiya.

Jane found a sedative with Bill's clear marking on the plastic container, took the prescribed dose, then slipped gratefully back into bed again, delighting in its warmth after the chill air of the pre-dawn.

She must have slept late, for it was a door banging that awakened her, and she started up. Looking at the clock she saw that it was nearly noon. The sedative had done its work and she pulled herself upright, then giggled.

Beside her bed was Baru's concept of a breakfast for this wife of his friend. Baru had often eaten breakfast with the missionary while on trek, and he had doubtless drawn on this experience to prepare one for her.

On a tray was half of a huge pawpaw, its orange colored pulp sending its fragrant aroma into the room. There was a dish of guinea corn porridge, now cold and congealed, looking more gray than ever in its pastiness. Beside it were some thick slices of bread, buttered lavishly, and beside them a jar of guava jelly that Jane herself had made.

Still giggling, yet touched at the thoughtfulness, Jane scooped out the luscious fruit, enjoying the fragrance as she did so. One slice of the bread with the jelly was enough, "enough for the two of us," thought Jane, folding her arms across her stomach.

When she had washed and dressed she went out to the kitchen where Baru and Kimbiya sat waiting for her. They looked like eager eyed children as they stood up and saluted her for the beginning of the day, as was the custom of their people.

"And," added Jane, "thank you for my morning meal," (there was no word for breakfast.) "It was wonderful. I ate everything except the porridge," she added not giving the reason for declining the paste-like substance. "I thank you a thousand times," and they grinned their delight.

The rest of the day dragged by, as Jane, unable to do any of her usual work and feeling listless, tried to read. She could not keep her mind on the book and soon threw it to one side, and sat, waiting with a feeling of impatience for her husband to return.

It was mid afternoon, and Jane was trying to sleep, lying on the top of the bed, and feeling the almost stifling heat press in around her when she realized that she was counting. Thoroughly awake, she lay there, waiting for her count to reach sixty. There. She felt it again, a spasm pain that seemed to knot, then quickly untie. She lifted her hand and looked at her watch, seeing the second hand sweep around the face every minute. And every minute she felt again that pain, each time increasing in its intensity.

She found herself amazingly calm. Sweat was drenching her forehead and streaming down until her loose dress felt cold and clammy to her back. Quietly she raised herself from the bed, undressed, and slipped a nightgown over her head. Then lying back, she tried to think.

Bill had told her that first babies were unpredictable, some delayed, some arrived rapidly after the first regular pains had begun. She must be ready.

Sitting up she called to Baru, trying to speak calmly although she began to feel panic once more rising inside her.

In a moment Baru was in the room with Kimbiya following. He looked down solicitously. She smiled up at him, pushing her wet hair back from her forehead as she did so.

"I think this is it, Baru . . ." She suddenly convulsed as another pain gripped her, and her hand went out in a piteous gesture. He grabbed it and held tightly as her fingers dug into his palm. She felt the strength that was there, and in a moment as the paroxysm passed she released his hand.

"You and Kimbiya will have to help me," she murmured the words, seeming to wait for the next pain and afraid not to be ready for it. "The doctor has shown you what to do," she looked up at him and he nodded. "Then we should be ready. And Baru," she took his hand for another spasm, then went on, "Baru, I'm not too brave. So if I scream 'you will know that it is just weakness."

"I know, **Uwar gida**," he was amazingly composed now that the need for his attention had arisen. "All will be well, with the help of God," and he added his '**Allah shi taimake mu**' with a note of deep reverence in his voice.

Then he barked an order to his wife, and soon the two were busy preparing for the birth of the baby, as they had been so well trained to do by the Doctor.

Once Baru left her side to call to one of the dispensers outside, but by now Jane could not distinguish the sounds and make them intelligible. From a haze of recurrent pain that seemed to well up and set fire to her whole body, she felt as though she was in a world apart. Now she was holding Baru's hand constantly while his wife busied herself near the foot of the bed.

"Bill, Bill," the plaintive murmur came from lips that were bleeding slightly from her effort to subdue the cries of pain that rose to them. "Oh Bill, I need you so . . ." and the words died away to a little whimper.

The mist grew deeper, and Jane had the awful feeling of slipping away. The slide was long, and below it seemed so dark. She could feel the wind rushing past her ears, and put out a piteous hand to try and stop the headlong rush.

"Oh God . . . Oh God . . . oh Bill . . . where are you . . .?" and the great black void rushed up to meet her. Just as she felt herself going, a strong hand gripped hers. From away off there came just one word . . . "Jane" . . . then sweet, blessed oblivion.

# XXII

Saliva flecked the corners of his mouth, and still Bill urged his legs to move faster, faster. The kit bumped and banged against his shoulder and back, and its weight seemed to slow him down. For a moment he was tempted to drop it for someone else to bring along, then he realized that the equipment in it was ready and might be necessary. He raced on.

Soon he broke into the compound outer yard, and chickens were scattering before his headlong rush. He was across the yard, had taken the small stairway at a bound and entered his home.

As he did, he heard a scream that seemed to bite into his nerve ends, and for a moment this man, so used to emergencies quailed. Then he was in the room. He grasped the wildly flailing arm of his wife, held it for a moment, then his own fatigue forgotten, he was bending over her.

Skilled hands lifted the sheet. He suddenly recalled that he was not sterile, and he quickly dropped it. I have just about one minute, his training told him. Feverishly he raced into the wash room, poured some disinfectant into a basin of water, took precious seconds to scrub his hands, rolled his arms through the solution, then with arms held up, bent at the elbow, trotted back to the bedside.

As he did so, Baru turned from the medical kit, opening a sterile packet. Soon gown, mask and gloves were in place, and with most of his minute gone, Bill was back at his wife's side.

There was no more time. He looked at her, saw that she was

panting with great gasping breaths, and in a moment he held in his gloved hands an ugly, red, puckered human being. It was his daughter.

Half an hour later, he was sitting at his wife's side, her hand in his. The pulse was strong and steady, her breathing low and rapid. He looked away for a moment, then felt a pressure on his hand. He looked down. Jane was smiling up at him through tear dimmed eyes.

He slipped to the place beside her bed, to bring his eyes and mouth close to her. "We did it, kiddo," his voice was husky and low. "We did it."

She smiled through her tears, and from far away her voice came: "The old firm, Bill," she pressed his hand as the words came from her swollen lips, "the old firm."

With a sigh she turned her head, and the sudden droop brought Bill in panic to his feet. He leaned over her, feeling the pulse, listening to the regular breathing.

"The rascal," he chuckled, "natural childbirth, and now she's sleeping like her own baby. God is good." Quietly and slowly he pulled up the covers to her chin, tucked her hand under, brushed back the hair on her head, then turned to Baru and Kimbiya who had already cleaned up the room and were now looking down at the baby that lay in the basket.

"**Mun gode wa Allah,**" Bara looked at his friend with pride. "We thank God for giving us this fine daughter," and he called her 'Titi,' the first daughter. Bill smiled at the 'us' his friend had used.

"We do thank Him, and as long as she lives in Africa she will be called Titi, because you have given her the name," and Baru almost swelled with pride.

Just then the baby, with its screwed up, pinky-red face, opened her mouth and gave a lusty cry. "It is hungry already," said Baru the professional, with all the knowledge of the birth of his five children now being presented to his friend. "Our people would feed her right now," and he looked eagerly at his friend.

"Not just yet, Baru," said the doctor smiling at the eagerness of the man. "In a little while after the mother has had some sleep. The baby will live without food that long," and he laughed.

Just then they heard a commotion at the door, and Bill and Baru left the baby to the watchcare of Kimbiya and left the room. At the porch Bill suddenly smote his forehead.

"I had forgotten all about you," he exclaimed as Dorothea's pain wracked face showed over the end of the stretcher being eased through the doorway, with Alan vainly trying to give orders in a language that the people did not understand.

Dorothea looked up. "It's all right, Bill," she said huskily. "How is Jane?"

"Fine," he was almost brusque. "A baby daughter." He dismissed any further conversation with a wave of his hand, spoke to the men who were trying to round a corner with the stretcher, helped them dip the foot end and maneuver it around and into the room where Baru and Kimbiya had spent the night.

Thrusting ahead of them, he quickly rolled up their mats, pushed their corn stalk beds and household items to one side, pulled the bed back to its original position, and placed Dorothea on the bed.

Dorothea looked up at them. "Thank you," she said it simply. "I . . ." she caught herself in mid sentence. Bill saw the sudden wrench of pain.

"I'll give you something to make you sleep," he said gently, "then we will take a look at those wounds of yours." He spoke to Baru, who was soon back with the syringe and small vial.

Bill turned to Alan. "Let's go outside," and the two turned, and followed by Baru, left the room.

Outside, Alan turned to Bill. "What a woman," he said in such a tone and with such admiration on his face that Bill looked at him sharply. "I don't know of any man who would go through what she did and come through it smiling."

"When we were getting her out of the plane," he went on, "it wasn't quite as easy as putting her in feet first. And without you there to give orders I had one awful time. But she kept grinning, while practically standing on her head as they hoisted that stretcher out. And it must have nearly killed her when the end of the stretcher caught as it was being lifted out, and she must have fallen a good two feet before the men stopped the fall.

"I was sweating blood before we got her on to the ground," he confessed somewhat sheepishly, "and there she was sweating, in dreadful pain, and telling me it was all right. What a woman!" he added for the second time.

Bill had known Alan for only a few months, but in that time he had realized that here was a man who had loved the thrills and adventure of flying, diving, or exploring the bowels of the earth. But never once had there been a whisper of a woman in his life. Unusual, as Bill well knew, for a man like this.

Alan's friendship with himself and Jane had been firm, good fellowship and mutual interests. Jane was sharing a rigorous adventuresome life with him, and therefore had been admitted to the cameraderie of men. Not as a woman, but as one of them. Now for the first time he heard Alan speak of a woman as something by herself. Again he looked sharply at the man who this time caught his glance and grinned sheepishly.

"You know," he started as if he had been asked a question, "I never had time or inclination for the other sex. My time and money went into things that I thought were more deserving of them. It wasn't until I met Peter Dunning and Ruth and became a Christian, that I knew that there was another type of woman to the ones I had seen. Then I met Jane, and I just accepted her as part of the package of our friendship. Then Dorothea, after all she has been through . . . well," he added lamely, with a grin at his friend, "there is a woman," and he turned away.

# XXIII

The baby was exactly two months old when the McAdams heard the plane landing at the airstrip. Soon after Alan put in his appearance.

He was very excited, and as soon as he had greeted them, pausing only for a moment to extend a tentative finger to the baby in her carriage, he burst out:

"Bill, I just took a swing over by the Kitta area and followed the river for a couple of miles. The water is low, the bank is flat and seemingly dry, and I was almost tempted to see if I could land on it."

Bill interrupted him: "By yourself?" reproachfully. "Remember me? I'm your partner in this."

"Oh sure," the other still spoke excitedly, "that's why I'm here. How about taking off early tomorrow and make a survey flight, then plan what we will do if we can land." He was as gleeful as a boy planning a camping trip.

Bill grinned at him. "Tomorrow it is," he assented, "but no landing until we have made all the necessary plans. There's more to it than just putting a plane down as you well know," and the other nodded. "There's also getting up again," he was deliberately being redundant, since he knew that they could court disaster with carelessness. The other nodded again. "Then I have to let the government authorities know what we plan to do and make sure that we have their approval," and he saw Alan's face go glum. "But we can make the survey trip now, then send word in to them when we see if it is feasible or not," and the other's face lighted up.

They spent the rest of the evening talking over the possibility of having this breakthrough to these totally unreached and comparatively unknown people of the jungle. Jane felt the twinge of fear that always came when she heard their frequently discussed plans about reaching the Kitta people. But never did she mention it to her husband. She kept it in her own heart.

The next morning they heard Alan up early, moving around the house impatiently, whistling in a sibilant tone as he waited for the others to join him. His excitement at this new adventure had awakened him early, and if it had been his decision he would have left at the crack of dawn. Knowing that a baby and a very sick lady were both in the house he sought to still his own impatience and wait for normal activities to begin.

He walked outside, saw the mist rising from the village, and the occasional plumes of smoke that filtered up from the all night fires that burned in the huts clustered there.

Slowly the village began to wake up, and an occasional call lifted on the slight, early morning breeze. Dogs began to talk back and forth, others clamored and joined in; he heard roosters begin their dawn patrol, and the occasional heehaw of a donkey now demanding its morning fodder. In a few minutes, the whole area was awake, and the noise spread to the comparative quiet of the compound.

He heard noises in the mission house, and turned toward it and walked in.

Bill turned with dripping face from a basin of water, and groped for his towel.

"I thought you were never going to get up," Alan chided him.

"You must have slept soundly last night," replied the other. "I was away for three hours attending a man who had been attacked by a hyena. Almost had his arm chewed off," he gave the information laconically, watching the other blanche for a moment. "So while you sleep, I work," he went on.

After breakfast they sat down with Jane to plan the survey.

"We should only be gone a couple of hours," Bill was saying, "and Dorothea should be all right until we get back. You can check her temperature, and if it begins to rise in half an hour or so, give her one of these," and he passed a small plastic bottle over to Jane. "If she is in any pain at all, some of that sedative I left for you should help. I don't anticipate any trouble with her, but you have done enough nursing with me to be able to take care of her if anything is needed."

Jane nodded. The fear that she kept hidden was gnawing at her again, and she didn't trust herself to speak.

With mid morning approaching, Alan suggested that they get into the air. Soon they had said their good-bys to the two women and the baby, and with Baru and some other men following, they began walking toward the airstrip.

"By the way, Alan," said Bill, "think we could take Baru along? He knows most about that country down there and he might be of some real help to us?"

"I think so," replied the other. "He will have to sit in back."

Bill nodded, and turned to pass the information on to Baru. There was a whoop of delight from Baru, and suddenly he was running ahead of them like a small boy.

When they reached the plane, there was no sign of Baru, until they followed the eyes of the men on the ground. And there, peering with delight from the rear of the cockpit was Baru, waving to his fellow tribesmen below.

Alan pulled the chocks out from under the wheels, motioned Bill to climb in, then followed suit. As the door shut, the crowd from experience suddenly turned and raced for the safety of the edge of the field, some standing there with hands over their ears waiting for the first staccato rumbles from this great bird that flew with men.

Alan checked through his starting procedure, Bill watching him in silence. Soon the motor took hold, warmed up, and Alan turned the graceful machine around like a ballet dancer pirouetting. It trembled for an instant, then in release was moving down the field and was almost instantly airborne as Alan gave it a surge of power to carry it over the trees. Behind them they heard the unintelligible sounds that came from the wide open mouth of Baru. The roar was still too loud for conversation, and Bill motioned to his African friend. The answer was a clenched fist, the thumb held upright, his tribal assent to something delightful. Bill turned back.

The country was rolling out beneath them, now jungle, now a great hill, then the occasional bare patch of rocky ground. In the distance, something glistening caught his eye, and Alan turned to him.

"The river," he only raised his voice slightly. The motor was now running smoothly and comparatively quietly. "We'll swing down, then follow it westward."

Bill nodded and turned to tell Baru what they were going to do.

Picking up the winding course of the river was easy from their height of nearly five thousand feet, and as soon as they began it, Alan dropped lower and lower.

At one thousand feet they would barely have enough clearance if there were hills ahead, and Bill turned to Baru to ask him a question.

"No hills," replied the son of the jungle, "it is flat like your table," and he held out his palm flat to illustrate.

Alan nodded and kept his height. It was easy to see the river with its brownish water, and they followed the twists and curves that it took through the bush. On either bank the mangrove trees grew right up to the water's edge. Alan was shaking his head in disgust, when suddenly both men saw it at the same time.

The river had snaked its way through a dense mangrove swamp, when suddenly it broke clear, and there stretching for about two hundred yards was a wide, sandy river bank, and from their height it seemed smooth and level. With a whoop of delight Alan brought the plane down to five hundred feet and they saw that they were not mistaken. It was the perfect landing spot.

"If there are any people nearby . . . ," said Bill, speaking the thought of both men. He felt a tug on his shoulder, and turned to see Baru pointing over his right shoulder. Baru's eyes used to peering into the jungle had seen what the men had failed to notice. There was a small cluster of huts, almost hidden by the jungle, and from them tiny figures were running back and forth.

Alan dipped the plane in their direction, swooping in low without thinking of the fear that he might instill. Bill spoke to him urgently; Alan nodded, lifted the plane up, and they were past the clearing, and it was jungle again. Before he could get the plane swung around to fix the position in mind Baru had pointed out three more clearings about the same size.

"Less than a mile from that sand beach," exulted Alan. "Closer than I had dared hope."

On the return run over the first clearing Bill focussed the field glasses on them, describing the people as he did so.

"There's one old man waving to us," said Bill. "Kitta people waving to us. God send us to the Kitta people," he prayed.

During the next few days they flew several times over the same stretch. Once Alan put some cloth in his bucket, and dropped it with his amazing skill into the small courtyard between the cluster of huts they had first seen. Through the glasses Bill saw an old man walk slowly to the bucket as it revolved on the end of the long rope. Then he dipped his hand in and brought out the cloth.

"It's the old man who waved to us on the first day around, I'm sure," said Bill to the others. The man looked up at the plane, then slowly he pulled the knife that he bore in the sheath on his wrist and dropped it into the bucket. While Alan reeled it in, Bill commented: "That's an African gesture. Gift for gift."

When the bucket was inside safely, the men examined the knife. It was made of a crudely smelted metal, its handle an ingeniously carved piece of wood into which it was fitted and held with leather thongs. They passed it back to Baru.

"**Aikin arne**," he muttered "the work of primitive people." Bill smiled. Five years before this same man himself was one of the primitives. Now he was helping them to reach others.

# XXIV

The little plane made several flights over the clearings, the men hoping that each visit would help to break down fear and strangeness among the Kitta people. The dry season was well advanced and the men felt that they should soon attempt a landing. Their object was just to land, stay in the plane for a time, then fly out again. If the people had the usual curiosity they would be nearby in the bushes, peering at this apparition. Once their fear had been overcome they could try to make contact. The men also would have to wait for a windless day since they would need all the plane's power for flying out.

Alan was practically living at the mission now, released from some of his other flights for this vital contact with the Kitta people. Dorothea was still kept in bed, although her condition had improved so rapidly that Bill felt that it would not be long before she could be up for short periods, and eventually could be flown to the headquarters for a flight home.

Bill and Jane were absorbed with the little life that had been given to them, and they spent hours discussing a name. "We have to call her something besides Titi," Jane was firm. Bill was delighted with the African flavor of the name itself, but joined her search for something that would go with it. It was Alan who gave them the final choice.

He was talking to Dorothea one day, and instead of using her full name, reduced it to the more conventional 'Dorothy.' Jane happened to be in the room, and suddenly she raced to the small hospital to find Bill.

"Anything wrong?" he asked, his mind going immediately to their daughter. "Is Titi all right?"

"Better than all right," replied Jane, "I've just thought of the ideal name for her . . . what do you say to 'Dorothy'?"

"Dorothy, Dorothy . . ." Bill said the name over a few times, "Dorothy McAdams. Say, it sounds good to me." Then it dawned on him. "Because of Dorothea?" he asked.

"Partly," replied his wife. "I heard Alan call her that a few minutes ago and it seemed to be just the answer. It is a lovely name for a lovely girl, and it will remind us that if she grows up to be as wonderful as Dorothea we will be contented and happy parents. Let's tell her that we are naming our baby after her. I'm sure it will delight her too."

"We'll make it official at supper tonight," replied her husband. "Make a ceremony of it and do it in her room. Don't tell her until then," and the two smiled like conspirators at the thought of what it would mean to the young widow.

That night they carried their dessert into Dorothea's room, and sitting there drinking coffee, Bill noticed how Alan's gaze kept turning to the patient, then hastily glancing away again, only to return when he thought she would not notice.

Then Bill stood to his feet and pompously cleared his throat. "Ladies and gentlemen, I would like to take this opportunity to make a few remarks. I would like to propose that at this moment we four should honor the youngest member of the McAdams tribe, by officially naming her and inducting her into the clan." He paused and looked at his wife and the baby she was holding.

"After much discussion and thought we felt that this unusual baby, the first white one born on this station, should be able to start life with a name of beauty, of courage, and we trust of honor. So Jane and I have elected to call our Titi by the official and registered name of . . ." he paused for effect . . . "Dorothy, in honor of our friend Dorothea Wald, who is hereby designated as godmother to the child." He stopped. Dorothea's eyes had filled with tears, and she had reached out her hands toward

Jane. Instead of taking them, Jane placed the baby in the woman's arms. The two men saw a suffused glow cover the face of the newly appointed godmother, then she looked up at the parents.

"The honor is too much," she said, "but since you have decided on this I can only pray that she will grow up to be a better woman than her godmother, that she will know the same joy in serving Jesus Christ that I have known, and if it is His will, that she be blessed with a husband and family such as I have had." Her voice faltered, and Alan, almost out of character in the somberness of his mood, and in one of the few deep gestures that the McAdams had seen him make, stepped up to the bed.

"Would you mind if I dedicate Dorothy to the Lord?" the question was asked hesitatingly. His spiritual life was not one that he paraded before others. It was seen in his constancy and willing service, but he rarely showed the emotion that now gripped him. As both Bill and Jane nodded, he put his hand on the baby's head as it nestled in Dorothea's arms and prayed.

For a moment his phrases were halting, then as he forgot the others in the room, he opened his heart as Bill had never heard him do before. It was a prayer of thanksgiving for his own salvation in Christ, and the joy of the new life he had. He thanked God for the friends that he had found. He prayed for Dorothea now lying so close to the hand that he kept on the baby's head, and Bill detected a new fervency as he remembered her in her need and in her loss.

Then in a prayer that started tears flowing down Jane's face and made Bill swallow a lump in his throat, he prayed for Dorothy, this new life with so much potential.

There were no high sounding phrases, no pretty speech made to the listeners or to God. It was the quiet prayer of a man who had come a long circuitous route to this moment and who seemed to fill and expand under the wonder of it.

There was a hush when he had finished. Then Dorothea murmured a quiet 'amen' and lifted her head to kiss the baby she held. Alan lifted his hand from its head and the three stood in silence.

The two men left, walking outside in the brilliant moonlight. It was Alan who voiced their thoughts: "Tomorrow?" he did not need to add anything.

"Tomorrow," replied Bill. "Is the plane ready?"

"Tuned like a watch," replied Alan proudly.

"Then let's turn in early. I will have to finish my medical work before we can get off, and there is a full ward in the clinic," and he nodded towards his small hospital.

The two men said goodnight, and Alan sauntered slowly up to the guest house that had been put at his disposal. He was in no hurry to go in. Thoughts and feelings he had never experienced before gripped him. He wanted only to walk and think.

# XXV

When Bill walked out the next morning he saw Alan coming from the direction of the airstrip.

"I was just checking a few things at the plane."

"It gets more attention than Titi . . . Dorothy," Bill quickly amended, "and that is saying something."

"She's my baby," replied the other, throwing his chest out. "I just haven't named her yet."

"Well, while you're thinking about it, let's get some breakfast."

It was past mid morning before Bill could get away from his medical work. He found Jane and Alan with Dorothea laughing at some of the antics of the baby. When Bill entered, Alan jumped to his feet.

"Ready?" and his eyes were shining.

"Ready," replied the other. "I thought we might pray before we go," he added, and Alan sat down again. "This could be the breakthrough that we have longed for for so long."

He prayed simply but fervently, then the two men got up.

"We should be back in less than two hours," said Bill to Jane. "You know how to use the radio," and she nodded. "In exactly one hour I will contact you and let you know how things are. By that time we will have landed and been on the ground for about ten minutes." He looked over at Alan who nodded. He leaned over his wife and kissed her lightly. Then with a wave to Dorothea, ruffling the baby's hair with his hand, he turned to follow Alan who had already left the room.

The two men had followed flight procedure so often that it was no time at all before they were airborne. Alan sat with his peaked baseball cap low over his forehead to protect his eyes from the high rising sun now flaming down upon this tropical world. His face shone with the joy of flying. Baru beamed from behind them.

The men followed their usual flight pattern and were soon over the clearings. For the first time since they had begun to fly over the area, there was no sign of life. It was Baru who ventured the suggestion that they might be out hunting since now was the time when the animals stayed close to the river and the water holes. Alan nodded, disappointment written on his face.

The men held a brief council, then Bill said: "I think we should land. This wasn't to be a real contact flight anyway. Let's try the beach for size, and it might be safer if there is no one around, just in case . . ." and he left the words hanging.

Alan nodded again, and swung the plane around in a great arc, dropping perceptibly lower as he did so. Soon he was following the river from the east, holding a course through the rift that the waterway had made through the giant trees.

Checking his landmarks, he dropped down lower and lower, and then with perfect timing they were nosing down as the wide stretch of yellow sand showed up immediately below them. The plane touched the sand, held it for a moment, then with full power was up and over the trees at the end.

As he circled back Alan looked at Bill. "Well, we can do it and the ground seems firm enough. I'm just afraid that we will need the full length of the beach to get out again. Those trees ahead are fairly high. But I think we can winch and push the plane back far enough to give us maximum running room. Shall we go for broke?"

Bill looked down, then faced the pilot. "You know your plane, Alan, so you decide."

Alan hesitated, then nodded. "Down we go," and he shifted the rudder bar and headed the plane on the same run that they had just taken. Bill watched in amazement. He was becoming familiar with the maneuvering of the plane, but he never ceased to wonder at this man who seemed to be part of the metal and fabric of his machine.

The run this time was made more slowly, and he set the plane down on the sand a little bit short of the first touch down.

"Beautiful," breathed Bill. "I couldn't have done better myself."

"You should try it sometime. It never loses its thrill," replied the other. "What do we do now?"

"Well, I had thought that we should just sit tight for a while and see if we get any curious visitors," replied Bill. "Perhaps we'll just wait a minute or two and then get the plane ready for a takeoff. You couldn't lift her out from here?"

"Not by twenty yards," replied Alan, coolly looking over the remainder of their primitive runway. "We would hit that tree just about where that crooked limb dips down," and he pointed it out to the two men.

Bill nodded, and he looked around with curiosity. The mangrove trees that grew to the water's edge gave a swamp-like appearance. But a few yards further back the dense and verdant jungle took over, giant creepers binding the trees and bushes together in an almost impenetrable grip.

"If we do get back here, we will have to come with machetes," he remarked to Alan and then repeated for Baru. "That would be the only way of getting through that bush." The others nodded.

They waited about ten minutes, then Bill remembered the radio contact. Taking the mike off the hook, he punched the button and waited a moment for it to warm up. "Plane to Jane," he smiled at the rhyme, "plane to Jane, come in."

"Jane to plane," came the instant response. "We're here. What's the news? Over."

"Plane to Jane," repeated Bill, depressing the button, "we have landed on the beach. No signs of life here or in the clearings. Baru thinks that they have gone hunting which would explain the absence of everyone. In a few minutes we are going to winch the plane back to give us more distance for the take-off. Then we will wait a while longer and see if anyone turns up. If not, we will lift off and come back. Pray for us. We will either see you soon or contact you. Be ready in half an hour. Over and out." He hooked the microphone on the little arm on the dashboard.

"I'll get out with Baru and hitch up the winch," Alan said. "All you have to do is ease this button in when I give the signal. Don't do it quickly or the cable might take my fingers off. Then when it is taut, I'll tell you what to do."

Bill nodded and transmitted the instructions to Baru, who quickly slipped out of the plane after the pilot. Alan reached back in, and from behind his seat pulled a long steel-cored cable with great hooks attached to both ends. Slipping around to the tail of the plane, he hooked it on to a winch that had been attached under the fuselage.

Playing out the cable, he and Baru moved back along the beach where Alan pointed out one of the great trees that stood close to the beach. Baru's nimble fingers wrapped the cable around the tree, then caught the hook onto it. Alan called to Bill, and they heard the whirr and clack of the winch as it drew up the slack, the lock falling into place behind each tooth.

When the cable was taut Alan called for Bill to cut out, and the noise stopped. With an expert eye, Alan saw the line of strain and tension, gauged how far back the winch would draw the plane, then moved to the cockpit.

"Now then ease it in slowly," he ordered Bill who was sitting in the pilot's seat. "And be ready to cut when I yell." Bill nodded, and the pilot dropped down and moved towards the tail of the plane.

"O.K." called Alan, and the winch tightened. Almost impercep-tibly the tail lifted and the wheels began to move backwards. The cable creaked, and the giant tree bent slightly. Slowly the plane moved back, pulled slightly crabwise by the angle of the cable. When it reached its maximum position and began to weave sideways, Alan called "Cut," and the whirring stopped.

Baru was sniffing the air like a hunted stag, his eyes wide with the intentness of his concentration. He was looking across the narrow river, and Alan followed his eyes. Nothing showed, and he turned back to examine the runway of the plane.

"Just do it nicely," he muttered. "I'm glad to have that extra running room, since this sand will slow us down," and he kicked some with his shoe.

Calling to Baru who turned away from staring across the river, he gestured to him to take the cable off the tree. Then they began pulling it off the winch, rolling it in great loops as they did so.

Baru seemed to be working with feverish intensity, casting looks over his shoulder while he did so. Alan, strange to the ways of the jungle born, shrugged his shoulders, and kept reeling in the cable off the winch. When it was ready, Baru picked it up, set it on his shoulder and moved rapidly to the door of the plane.

He reached it, and putting his foot on the small step, said something to Bill that Alan didn't catch. He heard only the note of anxiety, and some inner urge impelled him towards the plane's door. As he did so, Bill's head appeared.

"Hurry, Alan," he shouted anxiously, "Baru says . . ." his words were drowned in the great welling noise that began on the far edge of the river, rolled like a cloud and battered the ears of the men whose faces blanched. Baru was inside the plane in a flash, and Bill reached down to grab the arm of Alan, when suddenly he heard a thud and a scream. Looking down he saw Alan on the ground, a great, long hardwood spear jutting from the lower buttocks. Even as he looked another followed, pinning his thigh to the ground. He looked up at Bill, agony in his face.

Suddenly Bill felt himself pushed to one side. Baru had swung past him, using the top of the door way as a trapeze to 'fling his body outward. With one great pull that must have caused incredible agony to the fallen man, he had the spear that pierced the leg in his hand, and pivoting in a move almost too swift for Bill's horrified eyes to follow, he hurled the spear expertly back across the river.

In the moment that he had landed on the ground, Baru had seen a line of men break from the far side of the river bank, spears aimed. It was from them the dreadful, blood chilling noise had come. Now they splashed into the shallow water to follow up their advantage.

As Baru turned and with dreadful accuracy and strength hurled the spear, the men were momentarily nonplussed. The spear seemed to have bounded back from the ground almost as soon as it had hit, and these men of the forest had only one thought. Some magic was hurling their own spears back at them, and as one they turned and broke for the safety of the jungle.

Taking advantage of their momentary surprise from which he knew they would soon recover, Baru raised the stricken man to his feet. Blood was staining the ground around them, and Alan's face was waxen with shock.

"Quick, **Likita**," called Baru, "**Maza, maza.** They will soon be back," and with superhuman strength he raised the body of the pilot up level with the door.

In a frenzy of desperation Bill pulled, found the spear in the buttocks preventing him getting him in any further. Holding Alan with one hand, he gave an outward wrench to the spear, and heaved the inert body over the back of the seats, letting it drop unceremoniously to the floor.

As he pulled Baru in, Bill heard a thud, and through the open door saw the tufted end of a spear hanging from the fuselage. They were going to attack in force.

Suddenly he leaned forward and pulled the starter button as he had seen Alan do so often. With a thunderous roar the plane sparked into life, and as suddenly as they had come the men melted back into the bush.

"Not for long, **Likita**," muttered Baru, "they will soon be back when they find that the noise will not hurt them. Can you make this bird fly?" and he turned his great, wide eyes upon Bill.

# XXVI

Bill shook his head. "I have not learned to fly," he said in anguish. "The one thing we should have done we forgot about," and for a moment his heart sank.

Hearing a groan he looked back into the small compartment, now red with the blood that still came from Alan's gashes with every heart beat.

"You'll have to take it up, Bill," Alan mouthed the words slowly and painfully. "Do as I tell you, and we'll get her up all right," the last word ended with a groan that he could not control.

For a moment Bill hesitated, then he nodded. They might crash, but they would certainly die if they stayed here. Strapping himself in and instructing Baru to crawl back and do the same for Alan and himself, he began to follow the procedure that he had seen Alan do so often. His hands were steady, and he was amazed at the feeling of exhilaration that filled him.

"Do exactly what I tell you," Alan muttered. "I will feel what is happening, and all you need to do is let me know the altitude and air speed."

Bill merely nodded, and turned to his strange task. With Alan speaking so low that he could scarcely hear over the noise of the motor, he raced the engine, pulled back slightly on the stick, and eased the brakes off. The plane lurched forward, yawing wildly to the left. Bill's feet twisted slightly and the plane came back on its course, then was racing down the sand. Alan's anxious voice in the background controlled the novice pilot's hands. "Back, back, pull back," the voice was stronger and peremptory. Bill did as he was told, felt the tug as the plane lifted slightly, fed it more power and suddenly saw the trees at the end of the beach rush towards them. He pulled all the way back, felt a sudden jar as the wheels touched the tips of the trees, then it was clear blue sky above. Bill let his breath out in an audible sigh and looked at Baru. He was grinning from ear to ear. He didn't know how close they had come to crashing. All he had was admiration for this man who seemed to perform miracles.

He tentatively tested the rudders for control, moved the stick slightly to get the feel, and then felt free as he soared upward. When the altimeter registered five thousand feet, he eased back on the stick, felt the plane level out, then looked back at Alan.

The man's eyes were closed, and pain was etched on his face. Bill's heart constricted. The blood still seemed to be flowing from his wounds, but slower now, and his skin was waxen and glistening. His keen eye took it in, then he whispered above the drone of the motor. "Alan."

At the mention of his name the man stirred and the eyes lazily opened, blinked, then closed again. "Alan, can you hear me?"

The man's mouth opened, and a "Sure," came from the cracked lips.

"What speed should I travel with?"

"Keep it at about one hundred and ten," the words were almost breathed out. "When you get near the airstrip, let me know. Stay at this height." Bill turned back to the controls.

He remembered his radio contact, and with his free hand he unhooked the microphone, and flicked the radio switch. When the eye had lighted, he depressed the button near his thumb. "Plane to Jane. Plane to Jane. Come in Jane."

"Jane to plane," came an anxious voice over the loud-speaker, "Jane to plane. Are you all right? Your call is late. Over."

"Jane, listen to me. I can't talk much. We have had an accident, and Alan is injured," he heard a smothered shriek, as he lifted his thumb for a moment to ease the tension he felt. "Alan is hurt but he will be all right. I am flying the plane in and he is telling me what to do.

"Have some men with a stretcher at the airstrip, and get some blood plasma set up at the hospital. He has some serious spear wounds, but it is mostly loss of blood I am worried about. And don't worry," he added, "we'll get this plane down safely. God bless you," and without waiting for an answer, he added, "over and out." He knew that Jane would soon gain control after the shock and would have everything ready. He didn't think of not being able to land safely.

Soon the compound showed up in the midst of the dark green of the surrounding jungle, and he swung around it as he had seen Alan do so often. He felt the surge of power throbbing through his hands and felt the thrill that must have made Alan a slave to flying. He looked back at the man.

"What now, Alan? Airstrip is in view. I am approaching it from the east, and am about two miles out."

"Make a turn to your right and begin to descend," the voice was weaker now. "And don't touch anything until I tell you to," he added this time with acerbity. "Now start a gradual descent pushing the stick forward just slightly. Come in at this speed and try to aim for the east end of the runway."

"What about the flaps?"

"No flaps, no flaps. Just pull back on the throttle, and when you get down close to the ground pull it all the way off and fly level."

By a superhuman effort, Alan had raised himself on one elbow and looked through the windscreen over Bill's head. "Take all the power off now, then throttle clear back. When it hits the ground just let it roll straight. Don't try to guide it except straight." The misting eyes saw the trees ahead, felt a series of violent bumps, then the whine of tires as they whistled over the rough ground.

"Now the brakes," he lowered himself down again. "Put those brakes on easily man, . . ." the voice dwindled into nothing.

Bill didn't dare look back, but he could almost feel the fleeting, thready pulse of the man who had lost so much blood, yet had called on his last reserves of strength and skill to bring them down safely.

The plane was racing too quickly to the end of the runway, and Bill put more pressure on the brakes. The plane yawed, swung wildly, then stopped, just a a few yards from the trees at the far end.

Cutting the motor was the act of a moment, then flinging open the door, he climbed over the seat and knelt beside his friend. A froth was forming at the corner of his lips, and the almost stentorian breathing was heaving his chest up and down.

"Shock," said Bill to himself.

"The stretcher is here, **Likita**," Baru said. "Can we get him out?" Bill looked around for a moment, then remembered that the front seat was easily moved. Instructing Baru where a wrench could be found in the pocket behind the seat, and seeing him feverishly loosening the bolts that held it, then lifting it out and dropping it to the ground, seemed to be but the work of a few minutes. Then Baru was back in again, guiding the stretcher through the door, and together they placed Alan's body on the stretcher, lowered it where other eager hands reached up, and took it from them.

Bill dropped to the ground, then turned and began to trot the long path that would lead to the hospital. The men, urged on by Baru, and skilled as they were with carrying loads, followed. Soon there was only the jungle to hear the swift pad of racing feet.

# XXVII

Jane was standing on the steps of the hospital as he raced up. For a moment they looked at each other, then: "Oh Bill," and for a moment she was in his arms. "I didn't dare come out to the airstrip," she murmured, "I just stood here and prayed."

Bill held her off and looked into her eyes. "Then pray for Alan," he muttered, and turned and ran into the hospital.

In a minute or two he heard the men running with the stretcher. He was pulling on rubber gloves over his powder dusted hands, as under Baru's instructions and with Jane helping, they rolled the unconscious man onto the narrow table.

Bill bent over him, felt the pulse, rolled back an eyelid, then shook his head. It was a hurried gesture, but Jane saw it, and her hand flew to her throat in a moment of panic.

Bill barked orders. The men left the room with the stretcher, and Baru and Jane began their often practiced procedure with the plasma, while Bill worked over the man in shock.

Half an hour later, he lifted his haggard face to Jane. "I don't know," he formed the words with his mouth as though not daring to say them. "I just don't know." The two looked down on this man who had been such a part of their family for the past year, and whose life was lying in the balance. They heard a commotion at the door, and Bill turned impatiently. The words he was going to utter died on his lips.

Supported by one of the dispensers, Dorothea was walking gingerly into the room, her eyes wide and bright, almost feverish.

"Sorry, Bill," she said as she sidled into a chair with a sigh of relief. "I just couldn't stay up there any longer without knowing what was happening. How is Alan?" and she looked at the man whose arm was hooked to the plasma bottle and its life giving liquid. "Is he . . . ?" she didn't finish the sentence. She didn't need to.

"He's in shock and has lost a lot of blood," Bill was speaking with a low pitched voice. "I have managed to stitch the wounds. The next hour should tell us how he is going to do," and he turned back to his task.

Jane had moved over to the other woman, and they stood there with their arms around each other, seeking as women will, strength from one of their own sex. Their lips moved in silent prayer, as they watched the scene before them.

The doctor had turned away for a moment, when "Bill," a weak voice caused him to whirl around and in one stride he was back at the side of the man on the table.

Alan's eyes were opened, a faraway look in them, but a faint grin creased the corners of his mouth. "Pretty good pilot," his voice had the pitch of a tired little boy, and the two women leaned forward to hear him. "Give you your wings next time . . . on your *flight to glory* . . ." and the eyes closed and the head sagged.

Once more Bill felt the pulse, lifted one eyelid, then signaled to Jane. "Adrenalin, quick," and she turned to the cabinet. It was the work of a moment to make the injection, and the two stood by waiting with that sense of hopelessness and frustration that comes when one can do no more.

The lips that had gone white flushed suddenly and once more the eyelids flickered open with their tired look. Bill looked deeply into the eyes that now held his, and for a moment he saw them flicker. Scarcely breathing he waited, then the look came again, this time clearer and Bill let his breath out slowly.

Summoning all his skill and training, he reached out and held on to that flicker of life, while Jane watched. Every move, every gesture was that of a man who had often battled with death, and for nearly half an hour there was no sound save when he moved his feet on the cement floor.

At the end of that time the doctor straightened up, and Jane who knew his every look, raised her eyes to his. In them was a smile of triumph, and he nodded his head slightly. "I think so," he murmured. "I think so." Then he turned back to his patient.

Two hours later Bill stripped off his gloves and the short white gown that was splattered and blood stained. He looked at Dorothea, whose face had become gray with fatigue and pain.

Calling to Baru to bring the men in, he put his hand on Dorothea's shoulder. "All right," he said, not gruffly, but with a tired command in his voice. "It's back to bed for you. I only want one patient to look after tonight."

He forced her to submit to a stretcher, and the men carried her back to her room, with Jane following. Bill sat down to wait out the next few hours with his patient. As far as he could tell, the crisis was passed. But infection and shock have a delayed action too, and he knew that constant vigilance was necessary.

It was in the early hours of the morning when Jane had brought him some coffee that he again heard his name called. Setting his cup down hurriedly he went to Alan's side.

His eyes were open and looked clearly into his. "Thanks, Bill," the words were clipped. But the men understood each other. Strong men don't need a lot of words when they speak to one another. Bill's hand, laid with soft pressure on the shoulder of the other, was the only answer. Then the doctor checked his patient again.

Pulse and blood pressure were excellent, and when Alan suddenly asked for some tea, he knew that the battle was practically won.

While he fed the warm tea by spoonfuls into Alan's mouth, he told him that it looked as though he would fly again.

"With me as co-pilot," Bill chuckled.

"Not co-pilot," replied Alan, mischievously, "you'll have to take third place. I think the Lord was in that flight with us," and when Bill nodded, Alan grinned. "But you will make a good one when I can train you. You give me horseback riding lessons, and I'll give you flying lessons. Fair exchange?"

Jane joined them in time to overhear his last remark. "I think you have had enough flying for awhile," she said. "Bill, can't we get him into the house, where you can look after him and you get some rest too?"

"I think so," he replied and went to the door. Baru was sitting where he had been all night, waiting for the call of his friend. When Bill told him what was needed, Baru waved his hand.

"You and I can carry the birdman," he replied. "The carriers will be asleep, and when they are sleepy they cannot walk carefully. We will do it," and he thrust past the doctor into the room.

As Baru came into focus, Alan's eyes lighted up. "Baru," he said somewhat hesitantly, "**Na gode maka**," "I thank you."

Baru waved a hand to disclaim the need for thanks and walked to the end of the small, wheeled table.

"Tell him," said Alan laboriously, "that I know he risked his life to save mine. Tell him I'll never forget it."

Bill translated it, and Baru looked abashed and continued across the room without a word.

Bill followed, and carefully strapping his patient on to the bed with great webbed belts, he handed Jane the plasma bottle stand with its precious liquid, wedged other equipment on the bed under a strap, then with Baru at the foot and himself at the head, they easily lifted the load and began to inch their way towards the door.

Twice they had to set their burden down, once when Alan cried out when he was joggled a bit, and once to ease the strain. Finally they reached the house, and pushing some of the furniture to one side, they placed the narrow operating table near an easy chair, and a small mahogany table beside it.

"All the comforts of home," said Alan through stiff lips.

"For your information, that may be the next place for you," replied Bill, then caught his breath. The words had slipped out, although he had been thinking them for the past hour or more.

"You mean . . . really home?" the words seemed forced out of Alan's mouth. There was no laughter there now.

Bill shrugged. "We will see how you get along. Those wounds were deep and did a lot of muscle damage, and some repair work may have to be done that I can't do here. However, get some sleep, and we'll talk about it later."

Regretting his comment, he turned to the table, prepared a syringe and plunged the needle into Alan's arm. "There, that will give you some sleep, and tomorrow will seem like a new day to you."

He lowered the lamp, motioned to Jane to leave, then sat down until he saw the drug take its effect. The face of his patient began to relax. Lines of pain gradually erased, then there came the quiet hiss of deep breathing. Alan slept.

# XXVIII

Bill reached up out of the fog of sleep, as the sibilant whisper stirred him into consciousness: "Hsst, **Likita**, hsst, **Likita**."

Fully awake at last, he was out of bed like a flash, his bare feet hitting the floor in the running step that seemed to turn on the instant he flung back his mosquito net. In a moment he located the source of the sound, and was standing at the open window.

Looking up at him from the flower bed beneath the window, he made out the features of Baru.

"**Likita**," he said as soon as he saw his missionary friend. "Come down to my hut right away. There is someone you must see. Bring your medicines."

Without waking Jane or the baby, he pulled on his riding boots as precaution against snakes that would be out enjoying the cool of the night and seeking their prey, he picked up the kit that was always ready at hand, and slipped out of the house. The faint light of the moon was enough to show him the path that led to the far side of Baru's compound.

As he came near, Baru joined him. "We must not wake up the others," warned Baru, laying his hand on the doctor's arm. "There is much danger here tonight, and we must be careful.

"I was visiting up in the village," he went on, "and on my way back, I smelled something." In the semi-darkness, the African grinned. Often his white friend had told him that he could smell things when others couldn't see them. The doctor smiled with him. "I smelled something, then I heard a low moaning, and when I walked into the bushes, I heard someone trying to drag himself further into the bush. I shone my bush light on him, and there was a man who is not of our tribe." Baru paused, feeling the drama of the moment. "He has the face markings of the Kitta people," and he heard the missionary give an audible gasp. "I know their markings, and I knew that he was one of those who would have killed us the other day. For that reason, we must keep him hidden here, or those who love you might take vengeance into their own hands."

"But what is wrong with him?" asked Bill. "Was he wounded, or sick or what?"

"It is a wonderful story that you will hear," replied the other. "But now he needs your help, and I know that you would not refuse to help even someone who would have killed you."

Bill merely nodded, then pushed past the other, into the house. Lying on a corn stalk bed that Baru thought was the height of comfort, was the body of a man. With his first cursory glance Bill knew he was in a serious condition. His breath came in stentorian gasps. One arm hung limp and twisted, and Bill knew at a glance that it was broken, or even seemed to be crushed or shattered in several places. One side of his body carried great welts, and without touching him, Bill saw that several ribs had caved in to leave a great concave section. "At least four ribs," he muttered to himself.

While Bill worked, whistles of surprise kept coming to his lips. The man had been crushed and squeezed until it seemed that the bones of half his body had been broken. Perhaps one lung was punctured. He marveled that the man was still alive. Then surprise was banished. This was a man who needed help, and Bill called on all his skill to save the life of a man who may have been one who tried to kill him on the river beach. While he worked, Baru hovered at his side, handing him what he needed with the skill and speed of a trained nurse. "Better than many I worked with at home," he often told his friend to the latter's delight.

Dawn was breaking before Bill straightened up from his back-breaking position, to wipe the sweat from his forehead, and turn to Baru.

"That's all we can do for now," he said quietly. "He is still close to death, but the stamina of you people does what a doctor cannot do. He may live and he may die," and he led the way out of the room.

When Baru reached his side, the Doctor put his hand on his shoulder. "Baru, you said that your people might not welcome this man from the Kitta people." Baru nodded. "They must know that when that man came here in need, we had to help him. You must pass the word around that when Peter Dunning and I first came here your people did not receive us but tried to drive us out. But we did not leave you. We came with love in our hearts, the love of God. And we have this same love for the Kitta people. You will see that they hear that?" And again the African nodded.

"I know what to do, my friend," he said. "But when a man comes in at night, and is from people like the Kittas, then anger and revenge burn hot. In the light of day my people will listen," and he nodded his head sagely.

"What happened to him?" asked Bill, nodding his head toward the room they had just left. "He must have been squeezed by something."

"He was," replied the other. "Before he became unconscious," (he used the word for sleep) "he told me that he had wrestled with a python that surprised him in the bush. He killed it," he added, "and I will send my sons to look for it when it is light."

"Killed a python?" The question echoed with unbelief. "With his bare hands?" and when he looked his disbelief, Baru laughed.

"You white men. The bush to you is strange and fearful. To us it is home and we know how to live and fight in it. When he wakes up he will tell you what he told me." Baru turned to awaken his sons, and Bill reentered the room where the sick man was still breathing with that frightening, heavy breath that spoke of severe internal injuries. Bill sat down on a small stool, and began his vigil. A life, a soul was at stake. If his medical skill could be used to save both, this was his task.

# XXIX

He awoke with a start. Baru was gently kneading his shoulder, and with a grunt of surprise, the doctor jumped to his feet. "I must have slept," he looked somewhat sheepish.

"You slept a little," admitted his friend. "Now I want you to come and see what we have. If this man is all right?" he questioned.

Bill bent over the man. He seemed to be breathing more easily, and the more regular rhythm assured him that so far the man was holding his own. He nodded, then followed Baru outside.

A small knot of men was gathered in the center of Baru's compound, and they clustered around something on the ground. At the approach of Baru and Bill they moved aside, and Bill looked down.

Piled in ugly coils on the ground was the largest snake he had ever seen. Its body was thicker than his thigh, and the limp coils piled the dreadful thing nearly three feet high. On the top, placed there by an African with a doubtful sense of humor, was its massive head, with the great lower jaw, double-fanged, hanging down grotesquely. It was the only sign of damage to the great glistening length of the reptile.

Bill shuddered, then turned to Baru. "They found it near where the man was picked up by me," he said. He moved over and touched the great, slack lower jaw. "He must have killed it by tearing this down with his bare hands," and he grinned at the doctor, "then stabbed it here with his knife." He picked up the head and showed a gaping knife wound about a foot down from the jaw.

Baru went on, "The men will skin it and tan the skin as a present for you. We will eat the meat," and the men grinned their delight and coming pleasure.

Bill turned away. "I'd like to measure it first," he said to Baru as he walked away. "I'll get a tape measure from the kit."

He went back to the sick room, noted the man seemed to be still breathing fairly easily, picked up his tape measure, and returned to the knot of men. They helped him straighten out the gigantic snake, then held his tape measure while he marked off its length. When he had finished he stood up and looked at Baru. "Twenty-three feet," there was awe in his voice. "Indeed I would like to have this skin," and Baru nodded his agreement.

Before they stripped it, Bill sent a boy to call Jane, and she too stood in awe, and well back from it, as she heard the story. "And I didn't even hear you go out," she complained. "It wasn't until Dorothy cried that I woke up and knew you had gone."

Bill nodded. "And I'll be here for some time," he said. "Take one of the boys with you and send me back some breakfast. I don't know just when I can leave the man," and he nodded in the direction of Baru's house. "You tell Dorothea and Alan what has happened. I'll be in to see them as soon as I can get away." Jane nodded her agreement, and turned away.

It was late that day before Bill noted signs of consciousness returning to the man, and he hastily called Baru inside. "You can understand his language?" he asked in a whisper. Baru nodded. "Then when he wakes up you should be here so that he will know that I want to help him," and again the African nodded, then walked over to the cornstalk bed. As he did, he called to the doctor who quickly joined him. The man was lying flat on his back, his eyes wide open, his mouth slack. Bill knelt beside him and gently fed some water into the open mouth. As the liquid eased down his throat the man's eyes rolled first from the doctor to Baru, then back again. When a little water had been swallowed with difficulty Bill eased the head back down on the little, hard pillow.

"Speak to him," said the missionary, "and ask him who he is."

He listened while Baru did as he was asked, and heard the faint voice reply. "He calls himself by a name that I cannot translate for you," said Baru. "But it means a man who lives alone."

"A hermit?" the question rose in Bill's mind. "Ask him where he lives," he said aloud.

"He says that he is a Kitta man, but that he lives always in the bush where he hunts," came the reply. There was more of the hesitating talk, then Baru went on. "He says that he saw us fly to the beach that day and thought this was a bigger animal than he had ever seen before." Baru grinned. "Then he saw the men attack us with the spears, and saw the big bird leave. He watched it fly away, noticed the direction, and determined to follow it, and see what it was. Last night he came across it and saw that it was not a living bird, and was leaving when the python caught him."

"Can he tell us how he got away from it?" asked Bill.

Again Baru nodded, talked for a little time, then translated: "He said he was caught by surprise, and could not raise his spear or club in time to save himself. He said that when he felt the coils tighten he knew that there was just one chance. He let himself go limp as though he was dead already, and the snake loosened its hold in order to start swallowing him. As the coils loosened, he got one hand up on its lower jaw." Bill nodded. The snakes' jaws are hinged and drop wide open to enable them to start swallowing prey much larger than the mouth could normally take, letting digestive juices absorb what was too big to swallow. He was fascinated as Baru went on. "He tore the jaw down, and all the coils suddenly dropped away. He was able to reach his broken arm with its knife sheath, whip it out, and kill it. That is his story," and again Baru grinned at the man, as though to say, "I told you so."

Bill wiped the sweat that had gathered on his forehead.

"What a man," he marveled, "most people would have died. . . ."

"Tell him why we went to the Kitta clearing," he said to Baru, "and ask him why his people attacked us."

Baru's reply this time was shorter. "His people are hungry, and they thought at first that this was a giant bird that they could eat. Then they saw us, and I think they had the same idea about us," and Baru sounded almost abashed as he always did when he was speaking of some of the things his countrymen did. "So they tried to kill you." The man on the bed muttered something and Baru listened for a while. Then he turned to Bill and his face was alight.

"He says that he now knows that you are a man who will help and not kill," he said almost breathlessly, "and he says that if you make him well he will take you to his people if you want to visit them."

Bill nodded. "Tell him that we only want to help them, and perhaps we can see that they need not be hungry. Tell him also," he added, laying a hand on Baru's arm, "how we came to your people and brought the good news of God's love, and what it has done for you and many of your people."

Baru turned to the man and spoke to him for a long time. Flashes of understanding followed by looks of bewilderment chased themselves across the man's face. Baru then spoke to the doctor.

"He says he hears the words, and they sound good, but he does not understand them. He wants me to tell him more," and the voice was eager. "He also says that if this is what you want to tell his people he will tell them so, and he is sure that they will listen," and the man's face was alight with eagerness.

"We will make him better first; then we will talk about going to his people. Baru," there was awe in the doctor's voice, "surely this is what God has done. We could never have gone in by ourselves, so He has sent one of the men to take us in."

"This is indeed the way God works," agreed Baru. "Your bird-man will be happy to hear that he was not wounded without reason."

# XXX

Alan was sitting up in bed, with Jane, Bill and Dorothea sitting around him in a semicircle.

"I feel like a Roman Emperor holding court," he complained, after Bill refused to let him sit in a chair.

"So what is this family conclave all about," he asked suspiciously, looking from one to the other. "You look like conspirators."

Bill gave a self-conscious smile. "You're too smart, Alan, so we might as well tell you. I have two patients on my hands," and he looked from Dorothea to Alan, "and both of them need some attention that I'm not equipped to give. Soooo . . ." he gave the word a long drawn out sound, then went on. "I have radioed headquarters and they are sending out a station wagon to come and get you both," he held up a hand as he saw that Alan was going to interrupt him. "It was a case of that or have me fly you out," and he watched as Alan shuddered at the idea. "Seriously, headquarters thinks that you will get better faster if you are in the big hospital there where they can repair that muscle damage that the spears caused. I have also found that Dorothea will most likely require a spinal fusion. That knife went deeper than I thought, and she already knows that she will have to get attention soon at home. I was hoping that you might be of some help to me when we head back for that Kitta visit." Then he told Alan about the night visitor and the opportunity that they would now have of getting into the villages with him as their guide.

Alan listened with palpitating heart, and when it was finished, he whistled. "And I thought that that would be the last we would see of those clearings and the Kitta people." He grinned at his friends. "O.K. Doc, back to the hospital I go by that most plebian and lowly of means, the station wagon, but I'll be back so soon that you will wonder if I have even gone."

"We'll be waiting for you," replied the doctor. "But let me warn you that you will be on crutches for some time yet, but since flying in is the only way of reaching those people with the Gospel, I guess I'll have to wait for you. Anyway, you two can commiserate with each other on the way into headquarters. Your children will be there waiting for you," he added to Dorothea, "so as soon as a flight is available for you all, you can head home. I will send my report to your Mission office, so that they will have a complete history of your case. Will you come back again?" he asked as he saw the faraway look in Dorothea's eyes.

Alan felt himself holding his breath as he waited for her answer. Then he let it out quietly, although Bill's sharp look seemed to indicate that his trained ear had heard the change in breathing rhythm.

"I must finish the work that God gave to Max and me," she replied, looking up at Bill. "If it is possible, and He wants me back, I'll come." There was hope in her voice.

"What about the plane?" asked Alan, to change the subject that seemed to hold the four of them silent for a few minutes.

"One of your other pilots will come out in the station wagon and fly it back. So it will be ready whenever you are. Now don't look so painful," he broke in at the look of anguish on the other man's face. "No one will hurt your plane. I'm sure he is a capable pilot."

Alan grinned. "He's capable all right. But that plane is special for me so he had better treat her right. Now how about letting me ambulate a little so that I can help Dorothea when we leave instead of having her help the cripple," and he tried to keep his voice nonchalant. But for a moment he let his eyes rest on her face which was turned as she spoke to Jane, and his heart skipped a beat. She must have felt his eyes on her, for she turned, and briefly their eyes held, then she looked away again. Alan clenched his fist under the covers.

"Dorothea," he whispered to himself. The name sounded like music in his ears, and he let the whisper run through his mind again. *Perhaps*, he thought, to himself, *perhaps that was a flight to glory after all*. With an effort he turned his attention to what the other three were saying. But he only heard one word that whispered in his mind and warmed his heart.

"Dorothea."